ALL IN THE NAME OF
JUSTICE

ALL IN THE NAME OF
JUSTICE

A Novel

WARREN J. BRESLIN

Outskirts Press, Inc.
http://www.outskirtspress.com

Paperback ISBN: 978-1-9772-5351-4
Hardback ISBN: 978-1-9772-5366-8

Library of Congress Control Number: 2022907437

Cover Photo © 2022 www.gettyimages.com. All rights reserved - used with permission.

Outskirts Press and the "OP" logo are trademarks belonging to Outskirts Press, Inc.

PRINTED IN THE UNITED STATES OF AMERICA

Dear Readers,

A lifetime of work as a police officer, prosecutor, and criminal defense attorney has inspired me to write this novel.

My fictional lead character reminisces about his life experiences during jury deliberations that will bring a verdict in his latest and perhaps last trial—a trial in defense of a murderous drug dealer, one of many whom he arrested, prosecuted, and defended over the years.

The book examines authority—authority of police officers, prosecutors, and courts—and the need for a common-sense, practical approach to oversight that will check authority and assure proper governance. And yes, even private attorneys need to be mindful of their authority and responsibility to vigorously represent their clients and not rush to an expedient resolution of their cases.

Police need to be tough and feared by criminals, but not too tough. Prosecutors need to be fair and compassionate. Courts, prosecutors, and police need to focus on the spirit of laws—a fair application of the laws, application that would be conceded to be fair by all litigants. And all authority figures must avoid any appearance of impropriety. Equally important, there should be no smug tolerance of impropriety among the ranks of authority figures.

Authority must be well placed to work and get things done to serve justice with fairness, to allow pursuit of the ever-elusive democratic dream of "liberty and justice for all."

I hope you like the book. There are plenty of stories out there to fill volumes of sequels. My hope is that there is thoughtful reflection and progress in appointing the most qualified and effective representatives who will serve us all.

Thank you,
Warren J. Breslin

ALL IN THE NAME OF
JUSTICE

Contents

ALL IN THE NAME OF JUSTICE

About the Author:

Warren James Breslin is a criminal defense attorney in Chicago. He obtained his Juris Doctor degree at Loyola University after completing a Bachelor of Arts degree in Philosophy and a Master of Science degree in Public Administration at DePaul University. During his years of study, he began his professional journey as a city photographer and then a Chicago police officer before becoming an attorney and Cook County criminal prosecutor. Warren Breslin is honored to be listed in both the Martindale-Hubbell Register of Preeminent Lawyers and the Thompson Reuters directory of Super Lawyers.

While a third-year Loyola University Law School student assigned to the Chicago Police Superintendent's Office, he wrote and internally published numerous General Orders, Special Orders, Department Notices, and Training Bulletins. His duties also included speech writing for the Superintendent. He published an authored article, "Police Intervention in Domestic Confrontations," in the *Journal of Police Science and Administration (Volume 6, Number 3, September 1978)*, a publication of the International Association of Chiefs of Police, Inc., an article that was jointly reviewed for publication by Northwestern University School of Law. His Master's Thesis at DePaul University was accepted in 1975: *A Study in the Organization, Administration, and Management of Municipal Police Departments*.

About the Book:

Inspired by true events, ALL IN THE NAME OF JUSTICE chronicles the gripping and enlightening fictional journey of one man who went from police officer to prosecutor and criminal defense lawyer, exposing the underbelly of street justice, corruption, and the "blue wall" of complicit silence, all things done and pursued in the name of justice.

Authority without accountability provides little justice. This novel illustrates the practicality but dangers of authoritarian rule. Whether power is seized or given to those who rule, there must be further delegation of authority, with effective checks and balances, to hold authority responsible at all levels of governance. Authority can be corrupting sometimes, but it is necessary to get things done. After all, as we have been told throughout life, albeit sometimes unfair, "That's how it works."

X

Dedicated
to my parents in appreciation of their
motivation and direction in life's choices,

And to my wife for her unrelenting
inspiration and contributions.

Also, in memory of friends and
fellow police officers
Bruce Garrison & William Marsek.*

**See Author's Dedication Note Following Epilogue for
Death Notice of Bruce Garrison & William Marsek.**

And dedicated also to the brave people of Ukraine
and so many others who have defended against
inhuman dictators determined to prevent the
survival of democracy and humanity itself.

Inspired by true events, this book's characters and narrative are
fictional, embellished for reading enjoyment. Any similarity to persons,
living or dead, is coincidental and not intended by the author.

Prologue

We live in a world of social structure by necessity, to provide order and justice. Authority is given through elections and appointments, and often it is taken by force. Certainly, authority is power, and power can lead to corruption. There will always be excuses to justify wrongful acts, and sometimes those excuses have merit. The ends often do justify the means.

But it is the duty of populations to oversee their representatives and to act in the prevention and correction of corrupt behavior. Unbridled authority cannot be tolerated to reign if a society is to survive with justice, to pursue the ever-elusive democratic dream of "liberty and justice for all."

Warren J. Breslin

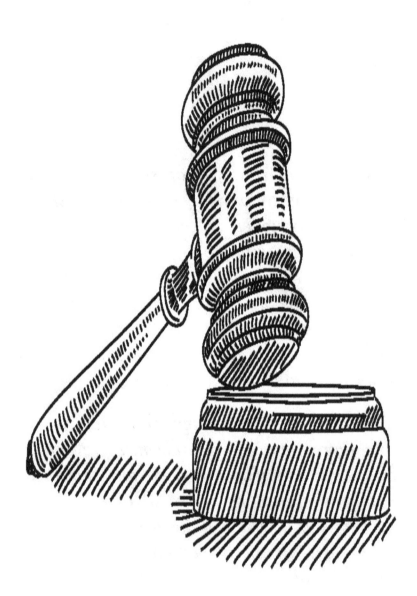

Chapter 1

The Last Trial

" **A**ll rise," announced the bailiff as the jury returned to the courtroom after a brief recess.

The court came to order and the prosecuting district attorney approached the jury to begin his rebuttal closing argument. Jack Keegan sat back, pensively reviewing each juror's expression during the prosecutor's remarks. The prosecutor recounted the evidence that was methodically presented during trial to convict Raphael Martinez of three counts of first-degree murder.

Jack Keegan was a prominent criminal defense attorney well known and respected by the most notorious underworld characters in Chicago and Miami, characters whom he had set free from jail time and time again. Raphael Martinez was one of those characters and the latest challenge to sharpen Keegan's criminal trial skills. Keegan had just finished his argument in defense of Raphael and now watched the jury's reaction to the district attorney's rebuttal argument as to why and how the defendant so brutally executed his victims.

Keegan sat erect but confidently comfortable next to his client at the defense counsel table. He wore his more conservatively styled navy trial suit so as not to jolt the traditional sensibilities of the jurors with his usual, more liberal, attire. His hair was thick and black with graying temples revealing the maturity and sophistication of a man in his position. His innocent deep blue eyes drew one's attention to his welcoming pale Irish face. But his exterior concealed a deeper, more complex, and cynical person.

The prosecuting DA, on the other hand, had not yet earned his wings of confidence. He'd just turned twenty-five—almost half the age of Keegan—and being fresh from his lifelong academic isolation had not begun to see reality as it really was. He was green to the corruption and influence of the real world that made things happen. But he was a formidable opponent. Keegan saw the prosecutor's naiveté as an appealing advantage to the

DA since the jury might reward his righteous efforts with a conviction of Keegan's client. His name was Jeremy Heitkamp. He was tall and lean with a Republican-flag-waving sense of responsibility. His hair was short and neat, his shoes shined for inspection, and his prosecutorial vigor was second to none. He was someone with whom Keegan would not now associate. The DA was "on the side of the angels," so they say—a comfortable and personally rewarding position that Jack Keegan was never to enjoy again. Leaving the district attorney's office, as Jack Keegan did years ago, to pursue a private criminal law practice assured one of a greedy reputation. For why else would one side with the miserable likes of Raphael Martinez?

Jeremy Heitkamp took his expected position before the jury and summarily reviewed his well-prepared notes before beginning.

"Ladies and gentlemen of the jury," said the DA, "you heard the fourth, singular surviving victim of this brutal and vicious assault testify that Raphael Martinez lured the four men to the third floor of that dark abandoned building under the pretext of setting up a temporary drug house. They were all friends, or at least members of the same gang, with a camaraderie shared by drug dealers working together toward a common objective of profit—profit which at their organizational level could bring in as much as fifty thousand dollars per day. Friendship in such a nefarious enterprise is so illusionary. Raphael Martinez lulled his drug-dealing compatriots into believing that the night would proceed with business-as-usual when, without giving them a millisecond to realize their fate, Martinez drew a chrome-plated nine-millimeter semiautomatic pistol and spewed thirteen rounds into all four men."

Heitkamp paused briefly to connect visually with each juror for impact and to assure proper attention.

The prosecutor continued,

"One of those men, Hector Diaz, barely alive, sighed, 'Why, man, why? Don't shoot me anymore; I'm dead already,' as he writhed in the massive pool of his own blood, desperately crawling to reach that unattainable place of safety, all the while knowing that his time had come to an end. Raphael laughed while planting his foot at the base of Hector's head and put his freshly reloaded nine above Hector's left ear. *Kaboom!* 'Now you're dead, motherf...er; now you're *really* dead!'

Raphael Martinez whispered to himself, never giving Hector Diaz a reason for his execution. He didn't have to, ladies and gentlemen of the jury. Gangsters like Raphael Martinez look at human life to be so valueless that there need be no serious reason to take it. In this case, however, it was just business, a power play to gain a better position in soldiering the distribution of drugs.

"Ladies and gentlemen, Vincent Vasquez survived to tell you of that last conversation between Diaz and Martinez and how Martinez turned toward Vasquez after firing that final fatal shot to Diaz' head and tried to finish Vasquez off. Vasquez made the unfortunate mistake of moaning after taking two in the gut during the first round of shooting. Raphael Martinez turned and stood over him at the hall doorway as Vasquez lay still on the cold linoleum floor pretending to be dead, all the while keeping his eyes open to see Martinez shoot two more times into his limp and helpless body. Still alive, but this time determined not to moan or move, he lay motionless until he thought all was safe and clear. Then, lifting himself to his feet, he made his way down three flights of stairs to the street where, as his luck would have it, Martinez was still there. Possessed with the instinct and the energy to survive, Vasquez bolted down streets and alleys over a ten-foot cyclone fence, took another bullet in the back by Martinez in hot pursuit, and awoke to recall that hellish journey while hooked to tubes in a hospital recovery room. It is a miracle that Vincent Vasquez is still alive to tell us what happened that ill-fated night. But it is even more wondrous that Raphael Martinez would sit here at the defense table asking you, the jury, to find him 'not guilty' of such heinous criminal conduct.

"You heard Martinez' defense attorney, Jack Keegan, make much ado about the credibility of Mr. Vasquez during his closing argument. During his cross-examination of our surviving witness, Mr. Keegan asked Mr. Vasquez if he were high on drugs and alcohol at the time of the shooting and questioned his ability to see in the dark. He would have you believe that Vincent Vasquez made all of this up or was somehow distorted in his recollection due to the very fact of being shot so many times or because he abused drugs. Certainly, Vincent Vasquez is no model citizen and lives a deplorable lifestyle, but he has the right to live and knows that the defendant tried to deny him of that right. He also knows that the defendant brutally killed Hector Diaz, Kendall Jones, and Ricky

Gomez. Despicable as he may be, he knows that because he was there. The People ask you to reject the defense's 'lack of credibility' argument and accept the vivid and truthful eyewitness account of these most hideous and brutal offenses. Find the defendant, Raphael Martinez, guilty of the first-degree murders of Hector Diaz, Kendall Jones, and Ricky Gomez, and of the attempted murder of Vincent Vasquez."

———

Jack Keegan knew all too well that everything the district attorney said was true. He'd met with Raphael in his office shortly after the murders, but before execution of an arrest warrant, where he sat behind his seven-foot dark mahogany desk with brass and leather inlay sharing a vintage cognac with Raphael while listening to his client's account of the incident. Keegan leaned back in his oversized tufted leather chair, undisturbed by the most gruesome tale, even congenial as Martinez delighted in telling him of how it all went down.

"You should have heard that dipshit beg for his life," Martinez proudly told his trusted attorney. "The hardest part of the hit was trying to keep my balance with all the slipping and sliding in all that blood. You should have been there. It was something else.

"Vasquez, the motherfucker, just wouldn't stay down," Raphael told Keegan.

"He was like the fuckin' Energizer fuckin' bunny; he just kept going ...... and going ...... and going! I chased him two fuckin' miles. I'm getting too old for this line of work. Maybe I should go back to school and become a lawyer like you. It's a much safer way to make all those big bucks; right, Keegan?"

Jack laughed condescendingly. He knew, however, that Raphael's equation of his line of work with Jack's law practice was not entirely frivolous. Just as his clients would prey upon their victims with no compassion or remorse, Jack's job required him to exploit the weaknesses of his courtroom opponents almost equally as mercilessly. And the consequences of his work could be equally disturbing. Jack would oftentimes have to reopen sensitive wounds that a victim suffered at the hand of a client. He would rip victim witnesses apart with his cutting cross-examination. Victims would sometimes leave a courtroom more humiliated and with less dignity than the emotional trauma caused them during the street attack. Jack reflected that he often had to deal with acquaintances' puzzled and sometimes contemptuous remarks as to how a lawyer could defend such criminals. He would retort with his standard textbook answer that every defendant had the constitutional right to be represented with the most vigorous defense that his attorney could muster. After all, would not everyone expect a defendant to say or do anything to get out of his jam? Jack insisted that it was his responsibility to do whatever he could do ethically to defend his clients. But it was left unsaid that there was a very fine ethical line that oftentimes had to be crossed in his zealous fervor to get his client acquitted. Routinely, Jack Keegan was defending the dark side of life. He had somehow established himself in a profession that rewarded him handsomely for winning the freedom of the most contemptuous individuals.

Raphael Martinez's comfortable rapport with Jack Keegan did not develop overnight. Raphael and Jack go back many years, beginning in the early 1970s when Raphael was a two-bit dealer selling dime bags of crack on the various street corners, attempting to dodge the police as well as the gangs who claimed those areas as their exclusive turf. Raphael always managed to handle the gangs, and Jack could always keep him on the streets. It became a mutually profitable business relationship between Raphael and Jack, although neither of them would consider themselves friends.

Raphael was a straightforward, no-nonsense kind of guy. He would know in a second if he liked you. And he would tell you to your face in just as short a time if he didn't. You had better be straight with him, too. There were many who weren't, but he didn't give them a second chance to double-cross him again. He wasn't a large man. He stood about five-foot-six and weighed one hundred fifty pounds. But he stood tall and tough in his daily underworld dealings, and everyone knew he would never back down in any confrontation. Leather, boots, and chains were a regular part of Raphael's wardrobe. Even Jack had a hard time dressing him up properly for trial. He grew one of those Confucius- or Fu Manchu-type three-inch-long fingernails on the small finger of his left hand. He displayed it proudly to all who recognized it. He used it to spoon cocaine to his nose and maintained it as a defiant symbol of his trade. He would not cut it off as Jack requested for the trial, but he did agree to bandage it to conceal it from the jurors.

During the trial Raphael Martinez sat next to his lawyer very still and expressionless as Keegan had told him to do. Jack Keegan knew from the start that he would not call Martinez to the stand. He knew that it was best to let the jury go without hearing from his client, not to reveal the coarse character of Martinez and chance an explosive confrontation during cross-examination. He felt that the winning move would be to argue the lack of credibility of the State's star eyewitness and convince the jurors that his client was not proved guilty beyond all reasonable doubt.

The jury received instructions from the judge and stood to leave the courtroom to deliberate. All rose in formal respect as the men and women left to decide Raphael's fate. Jack threw an arm across Raphael's shoulder in a sign of confidence and assurance to his client that all would turn out well. Jack Keegan had again fought so hard to win his client's freedom and now must anxiously await the jury's verdict. Remaining on a no-bond hold, Raphael Martinez would be escorted again into custody awaiting the jury's return to court.

Chapter 2

Recollections during Deliberation

The jury was deliberating for its second day. The jury's room was clean and comfortable, but not loungingly comfortable as might encourage the jury to linger in its deliberations. Chairs were straight-back and unpadded. Dark walnut suited their purpose just fine. No one dared discuss the sanitary reasons for keeping soft cloth surfaces from jurors' derrieres that might spoil fabric-covered seats. A pitcher of ice water was kept fresh on the jury's long table, and a water cooler was perched in the room's corner if preferred. Bailiffs would hover outside the room to be at the jury's beck and call and to take orders for lunch and dinner. Others waited patiently for the jury's verdict.

Jack Keegan was in his office awaiting a call back to court for the verdict while halfheartedly taking care of some housekeeping matters on other case files. Gazing across his office, Jack thought again about his occupation and remembered his father who had died so many years earlier and whom he'd respected so while growing up. His father was a Chicago police officer, a patrolman in the downtown First District for thirty-five years. What would he think of Jack's criminal defense practice if he were alive to see Jack today? Would he think like so many others that one had to be twisted to defend such monsters? Or would he understand the gamesmanship of it all with a perspective shared only by those who have participated in the criminal justice system? Jack reflected on his youth and on his life's experiences that made him who he was.

Jack Keegan was raised in an all-American, second-generation Irish-Catholic family of four. His folks were close and did everything right in bringing up their two kids. Jack and his younger sister attended parochial schools, took weekly piano lessons, and knelt straight during Mass as they were supposed to on each and every Sunday and Holy Day of Obligation. Jack grew through most of his teen years with an unrealized innocence so characteristic of the times. It was not until his very late teens that the seeds of liberal social change, compliments of the British music invasion and the Viet Nam War, began to take hold, causing mostly the youngest of his generation to question and challenge authority. There were gangs in those early days, but they were far less lethal in their rivalry, perhaps since drugs were not yet a popular commodity and high-finance drug dealing was not a consideration of anyone who "hung out." Fast-food places were their main meeting ground. They did not usually carry guns. Chains, clubs, and sometimes knives were always available for the occasional rumble. But fights were merely neighborhood territorial or racial brawls, not the big-business slaughters of today. They lifted weights to pump up and look tough in their black leather jackets and drove souped-up cars that sometimes competed on the city streets. Back then the cops ruled the city. The gangs talked tough, but the cops could scatter them in a flash.

It was great to have a Chicago cop for a dad. Jack was proud when newfound friends would discover his father's celebrity occupation. No friends in the neighborhood dared to discuss their dads' work as enthusiastically. Jack knew that his future had to be in law enforcement. It just had to be.

Jack's parents' plan for his future wasn't far from his own. They wanted him to be a lawyer. Even a teacher in the third grade told his beaming parents that he should become one because he argued so much in class—not a glowing reference for admission to law school, but enough to fuel his parents' hopes and encouragement that his mother would talk of that teacher's recommendation for years. Jack knew all his life that studying law was in his destiny, but he thought that he would merely apply his studies to reach his real vocation, becoming a secret agent or undercover super-spy in the FBI or CIA. He saw life in much simpler terms back then. There were good guys, and there were bad guys. He wanted to be a good-guy hero with exciting assignments to clean up the bad guys.

Jack was sixteen years of age when his father brought him to the neighborhood ward office to get a summer job. Jack's dad said that the alderman owed him a favor. It was to be Jack's first contact with the political arena where favors and political positioning were played like a game of cards. If you sat at the table and drew from the pile, you had better be ready to ante-up.

Grand letters of gold, outlined in black, striped the front window of the neighborhood ward office majestically identifying Rocco J. Calabrese, Alderman and Ward Committeeman. Jack was a bit nervous as he walked in with his dad and approached the alderman's secretary, a short, bald, potbellied man with an unfriendly look of arrogance leaning back in a seat-worn brown leather spring-backed chair with half a cigar stuck fittingly in the side of his mouth. "Sit down over there," the little man said without raising his face from the newspaper he was scanning while extending his index finger in the direction of about twenty folding chairs, half of them already occupied. They were to wait their turn in a line of other ward citizens seeking similar favors or to address personal problems in the neighborhood. The alderman was known to have great power to get things done.

The room filled with smoke as precinct

captains and ward workers gathered at the secretary's desk checking in after hours of political canvassing for an upcoming election. They all had the same sleazy look about them. Some whispered to each other out of the sides of their mouths while looking side to side as if there were some clandestine conspiracies afoot. Others boasted loudly of projected election returns for their respective precincts. None but a few could intrude to the back office where Alderman Calabrese was meeting one-on-one with his voters. When one did occasionally interrupt with a knock on the alderman's door, he would enter meekly, bent at the waist, with his head bowed in respect.

A man left the back office holding the door ajar for Jack and his father, who were next in line.

"How have you been, Jim? It's been a while, hasn't it? What can I do for you, Jim?" said Alderman Calabrese with an accommodating smile.

Jack was introduced by his father, who requested a summer job for him.

"It has been a while, Alderman Rocco, and

I am doing fine," Jim Keegan said with a modicum of respect for the alderman's position without losing his familiarity.

"This young man here with me is my son, Jack. He is still in high school but will soon be off to college. I told him you may have something for him during the summer, and he can help you ringing doorbells to get out the vote at upcoming elections."

Alderman Calabrese unexpectedly turned to Jack and asked, "Did you know that your father used to chase me around downtown when I was a bookie for the Mob?"

Jack was stunned. He smiled but could not answer him. Jack not only did not know about the alderman's former occupation, but also could not fathom why a man of his position would so casually admit it.

"I owe your dad plenty for the breaks he gave me back then; how would you like to work in the parks this summer?"

"I'd love that, Alderman. Thank you. What would I be doing?"

"Oh, picking up papers with a stick and wiping

down park benches. Nothing much to do."

"That's fine. Thank you again, Alderman; it was very nice meeting you," said Jack with a whole new perspective on his father's power.

Unwittingly, Jack was to become a new member of the Political Machine, a quid pro quo political empire under which everyone seemed to benefit.

Jack worked his summers cleaning parks until entering college. It was easy and temporarily rewarding with no future. Off to college at eighteen.

———————

It was in 1968, just before starting college, never remotely considering leaving academic pursuits for a permanent career position, when Jack Keegan thought it would be cool to be a cop—at least until the FBI or CIA would consider his credentials worthy enough for an application. He took the civil service police exam among seven thousand applicants for one of less than three hundred available positions. Being that the test was not that difficult, the real selection had to have been made during the applicants' "background check," where personnel officers gave the final OK after interviewing applicants' family and neighbors. Jack remembered the day two such officers came to his parents' home where he resided. His father met the two officers at the door.

"Ray, you son of a gun, I haven't seen you in a while. How did you end up with this assignment?" Jack's father quipped to one of the two.

"Well, Keegan, you know they gotta put us old dogs somewhere we won't get hurt," Officer Ray Kowalski said while turning to his partner and gesturing an introduction:

"Marty Cadogan, Jim Keegan—Jim and I walked adjacent beats in the First District for many years; right, Jim?"

Jack stood near but embarrassingly distant as an outsider to the camaraderie of the three officers as the friendly banter continued.

"I guess this interview will be a snap," Ray said reassuringly as he turned, winking his eye to Jack. "Don't worry about a thing, kid. You're a shoe-in."

Jack Keegan was "police family" and was accordingly given an automatic OK. He was to be sworn in as a Chicago police officer.

Jack thought he knew the job, having been

raised with the glamour and glory of it all his life. His dad, however, never brought the real job home with him. Jack stepped into a whole new world when he took his oath "to serve and protect" the citizens of Chicago.

"Keep your eyes and ears open and your mouth shut," warned Jack's father in a way that was more foreboding than advisory.

"And watch out for the four 'B's: *Bribes, Booze, Broads,* and *Bullets.* Those are the four things that will always get you in trouble. Watch and learn from the old-timers you respect, and you'll do fine," he said.

That's all. There were no other instructions—no father-to-son directions on how to be a good cop—and there was no professional coaching along the way. There was a code of silence that Jack's dad had never broken, not even with family.

And in one of the few times that Jack's father even mentioned the dos and don'ts of police work, he reminded Jack, "When you keep your eyes and ears open and your mouth shut, you learn to be a good cop and the pitfalls of being a bad one. Even when you learn the mistakes of so many, you plod along and do the right thing. You are not there to change others who don't. Cops need other cops. Respect the code of silence!"

Jack's dad knew that his son was about to grow up fast and learn that code as he did three decades ago.

─────◆◆◆─────

Jack scheduled his college classes so that his police academy training would not interfere. It was 6:45 a.m. on a warm summer morning when he followed an anxious-looking crowd of young men into an old, dilapidated building on Chicago's west side. It was Jack's first day at the Chicago Police Academy located at 720 West O'Brien Street, one block from the rat-infested Maxwell Street garment district where sidewalk shops and street peddlers would sell their sometimes-stolen wares to bargain hunters brave enough to walk the multi-ethnic crime-ridden area. The building was in such bad shape it was condemned years ago, but it served to train the troops—Chicago's future finest. Jack was unimpressed. He consoled himself believing that he would someday be entering the modern and well-equipped FBI training facilities in Quantico, Virginia.

"What the hell are you doing here?" Jack yelled from the doorway some fifty feet away, recognizing two old grade-school friends inside.

He had not seen Russell Congini and Mark Hagen in years and was not expecting to renew their childhood friendship.

"Jack! Jack Keegan!" Russ exclaimed as he turned toward Jack's voice down the hall.

Jack caught up and extended his hand to his two friends. Mark was beaming and overwhelmed with the excitement of it all. It was very exciting indeed to all of them anticipating the powers of their new office. The three of them exchanged small talk as they shuffled off together with the other police recruits to a gathering hall where they would check their classroom assignments and receive general instructions.

It was easily understandable that Russell Congini became a cop. His father was a Chicago police sergeant with some connections, and Russ had just returned from a two-year stint in

Viet Nam. Mark Hagen, on the other hand, had no police family ties and seemingly no propensity toward police work. He married just before taking the police test and left a promising future at a pharmaceutical company. Slightly less-than-average height but with a muscular build to compensate, Mark was considered very good-looking. He combed his light brown—almost blond—hair straight back and puffed forward in a fifties fashion. He had a smile and energy about him that was contagious. In fact, it was probably Mark's broad smile that people would notice as his most prominent feature. He always smiled.

Jack Keegan, as were all police recruits, being young, fearless, and aggressive, anxious to tackle any police work assigned to them, could not know what joys or tragedies might lie ahead for them. Remembering those early days, Jack felt such sadness for the tragedy that would befall his very close friend Mark Hagen. Jack recalled the joking and laughing and sharing of youthful times together with other friends. They skied in nearby Lake Geneva, where Jack took a tumble down the Playboy Club Bunny Hill and needed stitches to sew up a ski laceration to his shin bone. Mark jumped into action to drive Jack to a hospital emergency room to get sewn up. Back to the slopes they went. It was a good time. It was a hospital room where Jack last saw his friend a few years later. Not so good then.

Mark strained from a few people away to see the wall where the recruits' names, poorly typed and often misspelled, were listed in col-umns—groups of about thirty each.

"Look, Jack! You and Russ and I are all in two-o-one together. I see Gary Kosinski and John Holder are with us too. The whole damn neighborhood became cops!"

The reunion caused the young men to re-gress for a few moments of childish revelry. Their companionship gave them a sense of se-curity in their new uncertain environment. Then a lieutenant stepped up to a podium at the el-evated front end of the hall. The microphone squealed as he reached to adjust it.

"Congratulations, men," the lieutenant an-nounced above the muttering voices of the crowd.

It did not matter that there were eighteen women present among the trainees. Women in those days would ultimately be assigned to the Youth Division to attend to juvenile arrests and other, less serious situations. And the women were to be trained apart from the men, with their own room, with their own curriculum.

The lieutenant continued, "You men have assumed a position of responsibility that must not be taken lightly. You are the first line of defense against the uncivilized. It will be your job to know the law. It will be your job to enforce the law. It will be your job to maintain the highest standards of professional law enforcement and public service that citizens have come to expect."

The lieutenant continued with a general lecture on the dos and don'ts of expected behavior in the academy and then sent the recruits off to their respective classrooms to begin their training.

Jack and his friends with about twenty-five other young men entered room two-o-one and were met by a uniformed police officer that was to be their homeroom instructor. Although a patrolman and technically of equal official rank with the recruits, Officer Francis Murphy was accorded the respect of a college professor or a wise elder. Officer Murphy was to bestow pearls of wisdom and other valuable information that would help to transform those young men into trained police officers. He was not a man of formal education. But he knew the law and what it took to be a good cop. Approaching fifty, he could still hold his own in a fight and somehow managed to keep his belly and chin from extending like so many others of his years. Murphy looked sharp in his uniform. His shoes were always shined, and his shirts were always crisp. He set a good example.

Room two-o-one was like any other. It was sparsely furnished with about thirty old elementary school desks and a standing podium centered at the front blackboard. The large old windows opened at the south wall, allowing in a most nauseating constant aroma from the nearby Vienna sausage factory. It smelled like a slaughterhouse. Of course, there was no air-conditioning. Not even a fan. Even when the heat was stifling, one could argue the merit of leaving the windows open when an occasional breeze would only enhance the stench carried into the room. It was to be a long hot summer.

Before saying a word to the now seated class, Officer Murphy picked up a broken piece of chalk and printed two words across the whole blackboard:

"NEVER ASSUME."

Pointing to an eager young face in the front row, Murphy asked,

"What does that mean to you?"

The young man slid from his desk to his feet. "It means that we shouldn't take things for granted, sir."

"Are you sure?"

"I think so."

"You ASSUME so?"

"Yes, I guess I do," the young man said in an anticipated embarrassed response as Murphy pointed for him to take his seat.

"As police officers you must never assume anything!" Murphy shouted.

He turned to the blackboard with his chalk and slashed lines before and after the "U," dividing the word: "ASS/U/ME." In what he thought was a clever way to capture his audience, he pointed to his newly divided word and said,

"As you can see, 'assuming' will always make an ASS out of U and ME."

Officer Murphy had plenty more to say about misconceptions, and even weaponry, specifically police sidearms.

"Who wants to tell the class what to use as your best sidearm?" Murphy asked.

Few recruits volunteered to express opinions, especially considering the last illustration on assuming things. But a couple of gun enthusiasts could not resist the challenge to volunteer.

"Second row in the back," Murphy called out, not knowing the recruit's name.

"Recruit Officer Jackson, Officer Murphy, Sir. The Browning Nine Millimeter Automatic, Sir," Jackson said with confidence.

"Anyone else?" asked Murphy. "Right here in the front row, stand up, please."

"Gibbons, Sir. Smith & Wesson, .357 Magnum Revolver, Sir, with an S&W Centennial Airweight on the ankle."

"Better answer, Gibbons, know why?"

"No, sir. The Browning Nine is a fine gun."

"Then let me tell you why," said Murphy, prompting class anticipation of what was sure to be convincing.

"The Browning Nine *IS* fine, but it could be the death of you if it misfires or jams. Any automatic could misfire or jam. When you depend on the automatic mechanism to eject and reload, and when it doesn't, then you have no weapon to fire. You're dead. When your revolver misfires (and never jams, by the way), all you need to do is squeeze again for the next round to chamber itself.

"But consider the regular .38 models, or if you think you want a heavier gun, get the .357 but use .38 ammunition in it. Less recoil with less powerful ammunition allows for more accurate shooting. We're not shooting at tanks out there. The Airweight snub-nose pistols are fancy legwear if you think you can stoop to quickdraw against an offender while out on the town dressed for dinner. Again, recoil is an issue with a lightweight pistol. Stick with the regular-weight .38's."

In the thirteen weeks to follow, the three hundred recruits were to learn more than Jack had anticipated. Learning the Criminal Code of Illinois and local ordinances was a challenge alone, but the training did not stop there. The recruits were to absorb three large volumes of Rules and Regulations, including General Orders, Special Orders, Department Directives and Notices. Patrol Procedures, Investigation Basics and Techniques, and Psychological Workshop also kept them busy in the classroom, while a rigorous and often-times painful martial-arts class inappropriate-ly named Defensive Tactics—inappropriately named being that the techniques were very "offensive" in nature—kept them physically fit, but sore. Jack Keegan began to develop respect for the training he was receiving and for the men who taught him. He was no lon-ger taking his new job for granted, nor was he minimizing the difficulty and responsibility of the job.

Defensive Tactics taught the recruits how to remove a passenger from a vehicle without opening a door. A twist of the head and neck lifted a person from his seat and through a car window. His body would instinctively cooperate in lifting himself out. It works. Every recruit had to experience the pain of an unwilling but effective ejection. One hand under the chin and the other to the side of the forehead while twisting and guiding the body will take the body anywhere you want it to go.

Another effective tactic was the "finger grab." Grab the arrestee's fingers and pull them to the back of his hand while tucking his elbow into your armpit. He will submit and go anywhere you want. Amazing how pulling back even one finger will work.

Instructing Officer Charles Brandmeier gathered the recruits to demonstrate. "Jack Keegan," he yelled, "get up here."

In a fluid move to Jack's side, he had Jack's fingers pulled back and his arm tucked in so the two could prance around the room side by side with Jack walking on the tips of his toes. Brandmeier had complete control. Jack was in severe pain, but it was not really that visible to the other recruits.

"This is how to gain control of an uncooperative citizen!" Brandmeier exclaimed. "You don't have to bloody them up to   induce cooperation. Don't give pain-in-the-ass bystanders cause to get riled up and to escalate the situation."

Psychological Workshop was one of the most interesting classes of the training curriculum. It was 9:00 a.m. Jack's class had just finished a ten-minute break following a class in Patrol Procedures, and the recruits had retaken their seats. Two men, one black and one white, in shabby civilian attire entered room two-o-one and without warning pulled Mark Hagen from his desk, putting what was later learned to be an inoperable gun to Mark's head. The stage was set to instruct the class on hostage situations. It began.

"You owe us our money, Shithead. Pay up now or we'll kill you. You're coming with us."

The class was paralyzed, not knowing what was happening. It was the paralyzation that underscored the naiveté of the recruits.

Civilians are expected to freeze and panic in emergency situations; cops are expected to act. The purpose of Psychological Workshop was to expose the recruits to those situations and teach them to respond quickly and professionally. The course also served to weed out those recruits who could not cut the mustard.

Mark Hagen regained his composure along with the rest of the class once it was realized that his life was not really in danger. But it was an experience among others that would leave an indelible impression on all recruits and contribute to their professional transformation.

Jack and Mark became especially close friends during training. It became a friendship that would later change Jack's perspective on life and make him have a greater appreciation for it. They were only halfway through their training when they were called out as reserves in what was perceived to be the Hippies versus the Pigs Battle of the 1968 Democratic Convention. They were so proud in their new uniforms and expected that every decent citizen would give them great respect and admiration. They both wanted to be the best cops on the force.

When they arrived in uniform at Grant Park, across the street from the Conrad Hilton Hotel, downtown Chicago, they were jeered at by scores of longhaired political demonstrators. The likes of liberal activists Tom Hayden, Jerry Ruben, and even presidential contender Senator Eugene McCarthy were perched atop overturned garbage cans with bullhorns in hand inciting the crowds against government policies and the never-ending Viet Nam War. Jack felt victimized by the negative public attitudes that scorned his authority. It was a new era, and Jack was not to enjoy the prestigious position his father had held in Jack's youth.

But the seasoned police officers did not welcome the new officers with open arms either. Although volunteer Field Training Officers (F.T.O.s) accepted assignments to guide the new officers in their classroom-to-street transition, most old-timers did not seem to want to associate with the new guys. They had not yet accepted them into the real police family. All the police officers, old and new, were gathered in a makeshift assembly house at the edge of the park.

"Jack Keegan?" yelled a gruff field sergeant who was pairing off the recruits with their F.T.O.s

(Field Training Officers). "You will go out there with Fred O'Mara."

"Fred" was not O'Mara's real first name. It was learned that someone tagged him with that nickname from the Fred Flintstone cartoon character. He was built large and square and swung his club like a caveman. He liked it and even introduced himself as "Fred." He got a kick out of the subtle humor. Jack left the park assembly with Fred to hit the street. They were transported by squadrol to the ever-increasing gathering of hippies and police in the center of the park.

"You're Jim Keegan's kid, aren't you?"
"Yes, do you know my dad well?"

"We used to work together in the First District, you know, back in the good old days. A lot of time has passed since then. Things are a lot different now. You gotta be careful."

"More dangerous now?" Jack asked.

"Yeah, but I didn't mean it that way. People are different now. You've got the hippies, the pipe-smoking liberals ... more beefers. You can't get away with shit like you used to."

The squadrol doors flung open. Fred and Jack jumped out and took their places in the police formation. A couple of thrown bottles smashed at their feet. Something else grazed Jack's shoulder. Fred yelled what sounded like a war cry and pushed forward against the hippie crowd, pummeling every longhaired radical within reach of his club. All the cops joined in.

Nobody could hear command personnel, or even each other for that matter, to direct them in their skirmish. Radical protesters fell to the ground like swatted flies. Not many but some of the police officers were injured enough to be helped away for medical attention. Areas of Grant Park were set up by somebody to aid bloodied protesters. Medics from somewhere were there to help.

There is an art to using a police club—or the "baton" as it is appropriately called. Defensive Tactics taught the recruits never to swing a club from over the head to strike the offender with the broadside of the club. First, it can be grabbed and taken away from the officer. Secondly, it does not inflict sufficient injury to incapacitate the offender. The baton is to be always held close to the officer's body, arcing in a half-circular motion to strike the head, groin, and solar plexus with the end of the club, thereby inflicting maximum impact. Proper use also does not give an appearance of brutal force, as does the ineffective arm swinging caught so many times in photographs of mob confrontations with the police.

Jack and the other recruits were unable to implement their recent training, however, and had to just join in on the free-for-all. It was a great time for many of the cops. There was action that the rookies would talk about for weeks to come. It was an opportunity for the police to vent their anger and contempt at the liberal public that held the police in such low esteem.

Chapter 3

Police Days

J ack never heard his father talk about Fred and was not sure how well they knew each other. But that was not unusual. His father was never seen to be close to police "friends" and never talked about anything job related. The "job" was just that—his job—and his family was his world. Nothing was more important.

Jack had to learn the ropes of being a cop while working the job. He listened and learned what he needed to know. Young, aggressive cops were not his mentors. It was the seasoned, aging cops that showed wisdom and justification for all that needed to be done to be an effective cop. There was justification for everything.

It was Jack's first assignments that had him working alone, in a one-man car with a dashboard radio, rather than the later-to-be-issued personal radio, for dispatch communication. It was a busy weekend on patrol near an adjacent district when a citywide call came through the in-car radio.

"Shots fired at or near a bar at the corner of Montrose and Broadway. Any available units respond."

"Unit 2035 nearby," Jack responded.

No other units had yet responded when Jack investigated what appeared to be a quiet bar with no apparent activity. He entered to find multiple people shot dead, with their cigarettes still burning in hand, one lying across a pool table holding a cue stick, others slumped over the bar, of course motionless. Some were lying still on the floor. No offenders were in sight. All was quiet. It was spooky if nothing else.

The place looked like a wax museum. People had died in place, eyes still open with surprised expressions, all motionless, in positions that clearly showed their activities before they were shot. Jack remembers the scene with all the cigarettes still burning and unfinished drinks still in the hands of unsuspecting victims. Even the bartender was killed while wiping the bar.

There were nine victims that never saw what was happening.

Other police units arrived.

"What's going on. What do we have here?" exclaimed a police sergeant who then assumed command.

"There are no offenders around," Jack replied. "But there had to be multiple offenders or a couple of them with fully automatic weapons."

"Check the back room. Make sure there is no one else hiding from the offenders or from us. And put out the burning cigarettes. Check the bodies for identification," said the sergeant.

Keegan reminded the sergeant that it was a crime scene and should not be disturbed until evidence technicians and detectives arrived. Jack remembered from his training that it was his duty, being the first on the scene, to protect it—even from the highest-command personnel—until the scene was properly processed for evidence. The sergeant did not listen and sent Jack out.

Jack joined in the search. More shots rang out. They found the apparent offenders and exchanged gunfire.

"Secure a perimeter," the sergeant yelled.

Shotguns were drawn from police car trunks. No fully automatic weapons were available to the police, of course, to even the odds in their skirmish. With the perimeter held by some of the officers, Jack was then one of five remaining to do battle. He cornered one and yelled for him to give up before firing a fatal shot to bring that one down. Jack knew it was a bad guy since there was a spray of bullets screaming past Jack before taking his shot.

The other offender was also killed during the battle. It was then up to the detectives to follow up and discover the motives for the carnage. It was later learned that the shooting was prompted by a drug-dealing turf war among rival dealers—at least that was the motive to kill two of the nine victims. The rest were collateral damage.

Jack reflected on the danger he'd faced when taking that call and facing the uncertainty of the situation. It would soon happen again, however, in an incident that would sharpen his skills and wit.

"Shots fired," exclaimed the police dispatcher, "in the vicinity of Juneway and Jonquil. Units responding?"

Jack again accepted the call but approached the scene with more caution and observation to assess the situation. He asked himself,

Was the call credible? Any identifiable complainant?

Was anyone running or scouting his surroundings?

Were there other police officers in plain clothes on the scene?

Was anyone lurking around corners or peering out windows? Were they a threat?

Could this be a police ambush?

All were considerations that Jack needed to assess quickly. He did. A suspicious man appeared and questioned Jack about HIS presence. He was an indignant Black man who flailed his arms and screamed at Jack,

"What do you pigs want with us now? Leave our hood alone."

Although menacing and belligerent, the man was not a clear threat, but his hands went in and out of his pockets.

45

"Let me see your hands, Sir," said Jack, attempting to show calm and respect to the man. "Slowly!"

"Fuck you, pig. I don't have to show you nothin'!"

Help arrived that took the man down to the ground where he was cuffed and searched. No weapon was found, but a crowd was gathering that appeared even more threatening. More police officers were called to restore order. The angry crowd kept growing.

That night was very stressful. There could have been bloodshed. Jack thought, For what? A bogus or at least unsubstantiated call that resulted in a few disorderly conduct arrests? With all the arms flailing and threatening actions, people could have been mistakenly shot. Why do people not realize that police officers are just people too—doing their job to sort things out and keep the peace?

Dangerous calls were not the only real learning experiences for Jack. It was the conversations that droned on between police officers during everyday tours of duty—teaching experiences, nonetheless.

"Do you have a drop gun?" Thomas Kowalski, Jack's first seasoned partner, asked Jack out of the blue in one of those talks.

"What for?" exclaimed Jack.

"In case you need to justify a shooting," his partner retorted. "Wake up! Jack. You can't always distinguish a gun from a pager or something else! You can't always expect your boss to cover up your fuckups. You have to give him something to hang his hat on."

The conversation went on to instruct Jack exactly what to do in a "bad shoot" situation. Tom Kowalski stressed the importance to Jack:

"Never put the drop gun on the body, Jack. People may see you do that. Just inventory your 'piece' as having been recovered from the body so there can be no testimony later that you put it on him. You can't be judged for what people didn't see. Got that? And make sure the drop gun is clean—unregistered and untraceable—never to be discussed and never to be seen by anyone."

It made sense to Jack. The police are generally not looking to shoot if not fearful of being shot. But you can't always tell what a person is holding or reaching for in any given situation—especially persons who are agitated and noncompliant with police directives. It takes a split-second for a cop to evaluate proper use of force. If the cop is wrong, his or her life will either end or forever be changed. It is every police officer's fear that he or she will be judged harshly for that split-second decision.

Police recruits learned well that most citizen physical confrontations call for serious deadly force restraint when struggling with unarmed offenders that might use the officer's own gun against him. Police officers and offenders come in all shapes and sizes. You never know when an offender will overpower you. Only police officers, unlike the citizen review boards that judge them, know firsthand the fear of that happening.

Thomas Kowalski also commented to Jack about racial profiling.

"Don't let the liberal 'do-gooders' prompt you to lose your instincts, either. Ethnic profiling is an instinctive reality. It reflects life's experiences and observations. It is a necessary preliminary component of good policework and personal safety."

So those patrol conversations, and the too many street confrontations and shootings that Jack experienced, made Jack realize that "Bullets" were the most consequential of the foreboding four "B's" his father warned him to be careful of, not only bullets that may hurt you, but also those that you may fire at others.

Chapter 4

Perks of "The Job"

A s a young police officer, Jack was on top of the world. He was welcomed by every business owner who tried to bestow gifts and discounts on everything from restaurants to vehicles. His money was often refused at bars and restaurants that loved the police. It did not take long for police officers to justify accepting those gratuities. After all, it was reasoned, a police officer's presence in a business establishment rendered security to the owners and employees. Bars and restaurants, especially, had little fear of becoming crime victims where there was a plentiful police presence.

It was not just one or two police officers who advocated taking "freebies." The practice was pervasive throughout all police departments and all personnel. And if you did not want the bestowed gift, officers were expected to take it anyway so as not to discourage gifts to other officers. As one officer put it, "Accept anything, even a bag of crap. You can always throw it away."

Then there was the Playboy Club. Jack Keegan got to know the maître d' of the club's VIP room. He was newly hired from a hotel in France and afraid of Chicago's violence. Jack gave him a noisy blank-cartridge track starter pistol to carry that could scare off any threats, handguns being illegal to carry at that time. He appreciated the gesture as did Jack in receiving monthly issues of the magazine left at the club front door for him to pick up.

But the most impressive freebie Jack received came through the Playboy Club maître d' on Thanksgiving Day 1972. Jack sat down alone, in uniform, for a three-hour multi-course holiday "freebie" dinner in the VIP room. Bottles of half-finished vintage wines left by other diners were brought to Jack's table for his personal indulgence. Jack's "waitress" was none other than the October 1972 Playboy featured pictorial model, Lieko English who, like the maître d,' was also new to Chicago and agreed to let Jack show her around. Jack set a date for the next week but, as bad luck would have it, he was rear-ended in his "babe magnet" 1969 Mustang Mach 1 and had to cancel his date with her. Lieko went off with another admirer and did not reschedule with Jack. Oh well, it was still a great holiday meal.

"Freebies," however, made Jack uncomfortable. He had to work with partners who would spend a whole tour of duty shopping and eating. Donut shops were the most public "freebie" spots to draw public ridicule of the police that frequented them. McDonald's and other sandwich shops had officers come through the back door for meals to avoid public commentary at the cash registers. Jack refused to go around back for his meal but didn't criticize other officers who did. It was the way it was, and Jack understood the benefit of officers' presence at establishments but didn't like the unprofessional image.

For Christ's sake, how much coffee can you drink and how many burgers and donuts can you eat in a day? thought Jack. No wonder we are so often called pigs, Jack thought in jest. Pigs, he really knew, however, were a symbol of government officials hording the perks of office and sucking citizens dry.

So much for free food ...

Except for Jack remembering an interesting double-dinner date that he went on with a police officer friend who transferred to the 20th District from the 13th. His friend announced to the table that he knew the owner of the exclusive restaurant, the Como Inn, and the whole meal was to be free. It was Jack's first date with a young lady that Jack knew was sure to deny Jack any "late-night credit" for providing her with a free meal. Jack's friend had to be the "big shot" and turned an otherwise expensive date into another freebie handout. They did, however, have a good laugh over it and would talk about it for years.

Jack was happy to accept a desirable assignment to the 18th District, a high-crime district that included public housing projects but also tourist attractions and high-end housing, restaurants, and nightclubs. In the summers he was privileged to patrol the lakefront beaches on a motorcycle. Other times he walked Rush Street, the nightclub strip, and the Magnificent Mile, a shopping wonderland in Chicago. When he was assigned a partner for squad-patrol duties, he worked mostly with Kyle Richards, another young officer who loved to party—and what a place to work if you loved to party.

Jack and Kyle were a good team. They weren't afraid to work hard fighting crime but took advantage of "opportunities" that came their way. Kyle was tall, good looking, and comfortable dealing with the public. He was friendly and had his way with young women.

Jack was single as was Kyle. If they were married at that time, their marriages would have been doomed. You see, their district was loaded with young, available women who loved policemen. Sometimes it seemed any policeman would do. Although good looks mattered, it was a police officer's uniform and authority that were the main attraction. Women would place calls for bogus suspicions to bring police to their homes. Kyle and Jack, and others, would respond to find candlelit apartments with scantily dressed women who had very little to discuss but plenty of time to party.

Many police officers' marriages failed, as Jack witnessed during Jack's years of police service. Old-timers talked of being single again after three failed marriages. Others were known to have become wife-beaters and abusers—cause for dismissal as was frequently the case. Some became drunks who often failed to return home after nights of philandering.

"Well, hello, Officers," said a young woman who greeted Jack and Kyle to a bogus call for "assistance."

"Aren't you guys handsome!"

"What can we do for you, miss?" said Jack.

"What would you like to do?" she replied.

Jack and Kyle called in to stay off the air for a "personal." Their romp with the good citizen took longer than expected. They left without taking her phone number, knowing they would be seeing her soon on another call.

There were many available young women living at Sandberg Village back then. The residences were popular with stewardesses—or flight attendants, as they are now called. They were all young, mostly pretty, and trim, and females only, unlike the uninteresting mix of today.

Young police officers in the 18th District worked and partied hard. Often, they didn't even go home. It was so much fun.

Jack's alternate partner was Sal Amato. He was a likeable character who fancied himself to be old-school Italian. He would talk with mobster slang. Most people were "*oobatz*" (crazy) and had "*oogatz*" (nothing). He referred to pretty young women as "*braciole*" (which he pronounced "brajole") to mean an Italian dish of thin slices of tender meat. If you displeased him, he would exclaim "*bah fungoo*" (fuck you)!

Sal was married with small kids who were raised mostly by their mother. He did not spend much time at home; his second residence housed his mistress, or "*gumad*" as he would call her. It was a lifestyle to which Sal felt entitled.

Jack hung out with Sal quite a bit. They would stop at his home before stepping out for the night after their afternoon shift so Sal could shower and change clothes. His wife was used to Sal stepping out after work. She just stood aside in acceptance. Jack felt sorry for her. It was not what he would do.

"What do you tell your wife if she confronts you?" Jack asked.

"*Oogatz*," he replied. "She knows not to ask me about   anything I do. She knows her place and does well raising my kids. She knows that I will deny any wrongdoing anyway. Always deny! Even if caught red-handed."

Even his mistress knew never to ask him anything. He admitted nothing and did whatever he wanted to do.

Sal and Jack hit it off, though. Sal was fun to work and party with. Nothing fazed him. His always successful approach to women often puzzled Jack. One such time was at a small diner during work hours when Sal hit on their pretty young waitress.

"What's your name, honey?" Sal asked with a charming smile.

"Sue," she answered. "What's yours?"

"Sal, and this is my friend and partner, Jack."

"When do you get off work, Sue?"

"Eleven o'clock."

"Great; that's when we finish our shift. Do you want to go out tonight?"

"Sure," she answered with giddy enthusiasm.

"Great; where should I pick you up?"

"Right here," she answered.

Sal was taken aback and said,

"Are you kidding me? Aren't you going to take a shower and change your clothes? You gotta smell after working eight hours in this place."

Jack was stunned by his crudeness, but equally surprised that they later went to her apartment, where Sal spent the night.

Kyle was not as headstrong as Sal and later fell in love with a woman who Jack recognized as bad for Kyle. She was gorgeous and needy of things. She and Kyle would argue over Kyle's salary that could not support her desired life-style. Her name was Crystal. She encouraged Kyle to make more money.

"What are you doing with your life, Kyle?" she complained. "We can't afford to travel or buy luxury items. We are living like paupers."

"What do you mean, Crystal?" Kyle retorted. "We have more than most and could support a dozen kids."

That was not what she wanted to hear.

"Go out and make more money," she said.

It didn't matter that she'd never worked a day in her life. Growing up spoiled by her wealthy family—wealth that would never become hers—she was always pampered with whatever she wanted.

Kyle began "playing" traffic—a term used to describe solicitation of bribes to overlook traffic violations. Jack confronted him.

"What the hell are you doing, Kyle?"

"Trying to make ends meet, Jack."

"You better get rid of her before you lose all that you have."

And so it went with Kyle and others who crossed the line. They tried to justify taking bribes in traffic cases that would probably be thrown out anyway in Traffic Court.

"The traffic offenders are at least losing something by paying me to overlook infractions. It deters bad driving behavior and rewards aggressive traffic law enforcement. It is a win-win situation," said Kyle.

Kyle went down the rabbit hole and lost not only his job but also his needy woman, who never would have stayed with him anyway. She wanted Kyle to make more money but lost what little respect she had for him.

Crystal was one of the "Broads" that Jack's father warned of in his cautionary advice to avoid the pitfalls of the four "B's": Bribes, Booze, Broads, and Bullets. Whether through love or lust, women can motivate both strength and weakness.

Chapter 5

Stories from "The Job"

While walking the beat alone on State near Division, Jack approached a limousine driver parked illegally in front of a 5-7-9 Shop. He recognized the license plate HH1340 as registered to Hugh Hefner, who lived down the block in the Playboy Mansion, 1340 N. State Street. While engaging the driver in small talk conversation, out of the store came Barbi Benton, a *Playboy* centerfold beauty and who was Hefner's main squeeze. The driver scurried to the rear passenger door.

"I'm so sorry, Miss Benton. I didn't see you coming," said the driver.

"My fault," said Jack, apologizing for being the driver's distraction while locking his eyes with one of the most beautiful women Jack had ever seen.

Jack introduced himself awkwardly while being so mesmerized by her beauty. The driver opened the rear door while she and Jack spoke. What was said Jack could not remember. He was enchanted.

They drove off, leaving Jack staring at Barbie Benton turning around to wave through the rear window with a big smile. It was Jack's first celebrity encounter that he would never forget.

———

Jack was next assigned to a District Vice detail that included checks of business licenses and other possible irregularities in the strip clubs along Rush Street. At that time the feds were doing the same, unknown to Jack and district command personnel.

Jack walked Rush Street with a seasoned copper who had a personality and attitude not dissimilar to Sal Amato's. He didn't talk much to Jack, though, except for his positions on being caught by anyone for wrongdoing—

"Deny everything if confronted by anyone— even if caught with your hand in the till."

His name is not important here. Even his

marital status was unimportant and uncertain being that it seemed all coppers similarly played the field, doing whatever they wanted. He and Jack walked from club to club where drinks were poured, and strippers approached asking if they could do anything for them. On one such occasion Jack witnessed his partner, in full patrolman uniform, down a shot and allow a stripper to unzip his pants and give him a hand job—right at the bar while sitting on a stool with a broad smile (no pun intended).

"Come on, Jack. Lighten up. Grab a girl and relax. It's on the house!"

He motioned to a man overseeing operations and disappeared with him to a back room.

It was believed that Jack's then-partner collected "tribute" payments as "off-book" business operational expenses. It was learned later that the feds believed the same. Jack would not partake in the activities and soon left his short-lived detail.

On to real police work, Jack thought. He then worked the Cabrini Greene low-income, high-crime "housing projects" in a one-man car with a dashboard police radio.

It was not until much later that two-man patrol cars with personal radios were standard. In the meantime, it was expected that officers call for an assist car if required to leave the patrol vehicle.

———

It was New Year's Eve when Jack was patrolling at Division and Larrabee near the firehouse adjacent to the housing complex. Shots rang out, some striking Jack's car. He maneuvered the car to the curb and lay low.

The nearby firehouse housed firemen who were all too familiar with random shots taken at the firehouse from nearby high-rises. They were all illegally armed with pistols in their boots to defend themselves if ambushed during a bogus fire alarm. The police didn't care that fireman carried guns. They even encouraged their illegal carrying of firearms to protect themselves. They were all considered family who served the public the best that they could.

Buses were also targeted by gunfire. Citizens were huddled at bus stops in doorways where squad cars would swoop down with back doors flung open to invite and remove citizens to safety.

"Get in," Jack yelled to small, huddled groups.

He would drive them east to safety and return for the next group.

Naïve out-of-town visitors east of there at the bars and clubs would sometimes ask if there were fireworks nearby. Jack just smiled without answering and wished them a Happy New Year.

This happened in the "projects" every New Year's Eve and Fourth of July. Gunshots and explosives (M-80s and "who knows what else?") were popular party favors in the area. All calls for police response to housing project residences were ignored until after "celebrations" subsided. But Jack and other officers carried boxes of extra ammunition with them in case they got pinned down.

One night Jack was off-duty at a Rush Street Bar, appropriately named "The Snake Pit." He was with his lifelong friend and fellow police officer Russ Congini, consuming more alcohol than he should have been while armed with a firearm. It was required that police officers in Chicago always carry their police identification and firearms, even off-duty, so they could react to protect persons and property when their service was needed. It was difficult to comply with the requirement to jump into action off-duty, however, being that it was also a requirement never to be drunk or impaired, and especially when most officers were known to party and imbibe to excess.

While sitting on stools at the Snake Pit bar, their backs to the door, as known by officers never to position themselves for safety awareness, a robber came in and tucked a sawed-off shotgun between the shoulders of Jack and Russ and demanded cash from the bartender, who was staring down the shotgun barrel. Jack was about to grab the gun barrel but realized the bartender could be shot and the heat from the blast could cause Jack to let go of the hot barrel and endanger himself and others even more. The robber ran out with the cash and Jack ran after. Russ was close behind.

Jack pulled his .45-caliber Colt Commander from his waistband and attempted to pump a hollow-point cartridge into the chamber. He forgot that he always kept a cartridge loaded into the chamber and only needed to unlock and squeeze the trigger to discharge the weapon. Unnecessarily pulling back the slide to feed one into the chamber, Jack's gun jammed with the unspent hollow-point cartridge hanging up in the ejection chamber. While trying to clear the jam, the robber ran far away, leaving Jack fiddling with his gun at the entrance to the bar. A two-man squad car responding to the robbery swept in with the passenger officer jumping out to stick a gun into Jack's stomach. The police officer driving the squad car recognized Jack to be a fellow officer and yelled loudly to his partner, "He's a cop! He's one of us."

The robber escaped with the cash, but more importantly Jack escaped with his life. Being that Jack was lightheaded from drinking and no shots were fired, Jack's presence and involvement were not included in the responding officers' report.

Both Jack Keegan and Russ Congini just stared at each other in shock, both remembering the wise warnings from their training homeroom instructor, Officer Murphy: "Carry a reliable revolver. Automatics jam and can get you killed."

Dangerous policework was a young man's job. Not even ten percent of the street-assigned police officers exposed themselves unnecessarily to danger. Older officers took nonhazardous details whenever they became available. Young, aggressive officers and tactical units did most of the hard work.

—————

But police work was not always dangerous. It was many times more humorous than it was hazardous.

Jack's face broke into a broad smile thinking about a dirty young hillbilly street prostitute nick-named "Mailbox Marilyn." She was an all-night, every-night skin peddler working the Uptown streets of the 20th District. She was filthy all the time. She was a street girl doing the best she could.

Few teeth and a tattered short dress with noth-ing underneath, Jack could not remember a more interesting prostitute than Mailbox Marilyn. Who would pay for sex with that girl? Jack thought. Most would be surprised. She had more money stashed away than most coppers ever dreamed of.

Marilyn was an enterprising woman who car-ried self-addressed stamped envelopes with her before roaming the streets for her horny prey. Drivers would swoop to the curb for a quickie, and she would mail the cash payment immediately to herself in her pre-addressed envelopes, so as not to have the money snatched away from her by her tricks or jealous competition.

Marilyn would be arrested almost every night, but she was often given a few more hours to make her quota before being tucked in at the district lockup. She only objected to her arrest when business was slow. Otherwise, she would welcome the respite.

———————

Then there was a bum. A homeless, transient bum Jack Keegan learned to be more than that. He was somebody. He was a once-respected person who was being transported to the station lockup for the night. He surprised Jack and his partner with a voice that resounded his past with a story of abuse and addiction that clouded his significant social contribution as a once college professor and family man who became despondent and lost in alcohol, lost in his life of loveless depression.

"You don't know me," he said. "I used to be young. I used to have a life worth living just like you. Don't think you're better than I am. Don't think you're any different than the people you meet and scoff at in your smugness, with your indifference. We are the same. We are just taking different paths to our same destinies of death, no better than the next who will meet the same fate. Nobody ever grew up wanting or expecting to be a bum."

Being a policeman was a true study of humanity. The stories of cops could fill volumes of books. The stories were often repeated among friends and coworkers, but none were to be shared with family. A cop was ever mindful of the police code of silence, not only to protect fellow cops, but also to insulate their families from the depravity of humanity.

The most humorous stories, it seemed, were not funny to some and most inappropriate to share—like the homeless drunks that were stripped naked and hosed down by the wagon transport cops before being taken into the station for the night, like the gangbangers who were made to stand in alleys with apples to be shot from the tops of their heads for target practice, or like citizens who asked directions and were sent miles out of their way in the wrong direction. Not funny at all now, Jack thought, not even funny then. But he laughed with the rest of the young cops when it was the sick humor of the day. Too bad maturity takes so long.

Cops did often act badly, but they were feared, if not respected. There was more order in society with the unpredictable behavior of cops. It seems cops' hands are so tied today that they can't do their job. They are often perceived to be weak and feckless, at least by the criminals, as we hear so much from victims of violence blaming cops for being either too abusive or too ineffective. The daily news interviews of citizens blaming the police for their plight overshadows the unreported neglected responsibilities of citizens to embrace moral social behavior. "Mutual respect and responsibilities" are a two-way street.

"No-Knock" warrants allowing officers to break down doors in the middle of the night were always a recipe for sad consequences, Jack thought, being that any good citizen would grab a gun to defend against such an intrusion. But police must never be restricted from exercising their use of deadly force in situations allowed by law, especially in situations to apprehend fleeing forcible felons. Discouraging police from doing their job leaves us all unprotected. And media interviews of citizens who do not understand or respect police powers under the law propagate irresponsible reporting that discourages police from doing what they need to do.

Jack Keegan soon learned that, without good common-sense discretion, lawful enforcement of our laws did not always bring equitable justice.

It was in the 1970s when the Chicago Police Department started a program to improve public relations by implementing the "Officer Friendly" image where police officers, with that label replacing their uniform nametag, were assigned to schools to develop a better rapport with kids that would hopefully someday change public attitudes and perception of police officers. In Jack Keegan's view it was merely false propaganda designed to lull people to believe that police officers were friends. They were not, nor was it their job to be friends. Many, if not most, were friendly, but their job was law enforcement that didn't involve cozying up to be buddies with people that might someday be targets of criminal investigations.

In fact, the isolated separation of police officers

from the general public is felt so strongly by police officers that many do not take the stress of the job well. Tremendous responsibility to make life-and-death decisions and to solve the problems of others overburden some enough to commit suicide. It is a fact that police officers, more than in any other occupation, commit suicide all too often. It is a dubious, mentally unstable occurrence that is shared with doctors and dentists, who do not fall far behind statistically.

Keegan remembered a case where the parents of a seventeen-year-old boy suspected him to be involved with illegal drugs. He was disobedient and even incorrigible to the point where his father called the "friendly officers" for them to render their help to straighten their son out. A patrol officer responded to the parents' call.

"How can we help you, Mr. and Mrs. Jones?" asked the beat cop. Circumstances were explained, and the officer sent his report to the Vice Control Division for follow-up. A VCD narcotics officer responded to interview the parents.

"What makes you think that your son is messing around with drugs?" he asked.

"He's out all nights up to no good with his

no-good friends. We just know he is involved with something he shouldn't be," Mr. Jones responded.

"Have you ever been around illegal drugs to have knowledge of the signs of drug abuse or dealing? And does your son know if you did?"

"We talked openly with him that we used to be around marijuana in the early to mid-'60s," said the father embarrassingly of old times. "Why?"

"Here's what we'll do, Mr. and Mrs. Jones. You will introduce me to your son as an old friend from your past who asked if you knew of anyone who could provide me with drugs. We'll see where it goes from there. Okay?"

The parents agreed and called their son to meet up at the house. The son was introduced to the undercover officer as an old friend looking for drugs, any kind of drugs for recreational use. The boy at first said he didn't know of anyone who could provide him with anything but, to appear cool to his parents and their friend, he agreed to ask around. He was able to find an acquaintance who had a bag of "Ecstasy." Ecstasy, also known as "Molly," is a synthetic drug known to cause hallucinogenic and stimulant effects.

The time and place were set to deliver twenty tabs of the drug for a price unremembered by Jack. The boys came to the house of the Jones boy for the transaction. The Jones boy introduced his acquaintance/friend to the undercover cop, and the deal went down. Both boys were arrested and charged to face a class-X felony prosecution that carried a mandatory penitentiary sentence of six to thirty years for delivery of just fifteen of those twenty tablets to the undercover officer.

"No! No! No!" exclaimed Mrs. Jones. "This is not what we wanted. Wait! Wait! What are you doing this for?"

Other officers stormed into the house after being given the signal. "Move aside, Ma'am," said one of the officers, who began a search of the house for other contraband. The two boys were taken to the floor, where they were searched and cuffed behind their backs. They were then lifted to their feet by the handcuffs and brought to the awaiting squadrol for transportation to the lockup. The house furniture and belongings were ripped apart to no other consequence but the humiliation and despair of jaw-dropped parents sobbing with regret.

The Jones family was devastated and torn apart by what was meant to be an enlightenment to the parents of their son's activities so they could take the necessary parental disciplinary action to correct his behavior. And their son barely knew the dealing boy.

"Shame on the police for setting up a young boy whose life will forever change," Jack thought and expressed to the arresting officer. Jack knew that at age seventeen the boy was an adult under Illinois criminal law and would be serving his lengthy prison sentence as an inmate "bitch."

Jack learned that after an entrapment defense failed, causing the case to be lost, the sentencing judge had no power to sentence both boys to less than the six-year minimum. The boys were sent downstate to the same penitentiary. At every family visit, the boys pleaded for more and more money to be sent to the commissary for their purchase of cartons and cartons of cigarettes, surprisingly needed because neither of the boys smoked. After a while, anxiety in the boys diminished to hopelessness. They no longer needed to buy cigarettes. Hopelessness also consumed their parents, who could not do more to help.

Mr. and Mrs. Jones divorced after many disappointing months, being helpless to protect their only child from being regularly abused in custody.

Mr. Jones drank himself into despondency and put a gun to the roof of his mouth. The devastating news of the family's tragic end did not even move the arresting officer to speak remorseful words and show sorrow for the result. Jack wished it would have been that officer who put the gun to his mouth.

———∼∼∼———

The illegal drug business was and always will be a booming enterprise. It was difficult to know the players being that it is all about big money and all profit. Small players and recreational players are seen to fuel the big drug business and so must be taken down along with the major dealers to curtail the illegal drug use epidemic. It was difficult and sometimes impossible for police officers to distinguish who was using recreationally and who was in deep. Narcotics investigations sometimes even led to elected officials and government workers, and to police officers as well.

Keegan recalled a major DEA arrest of three Chicago suburban police officers freelancing to steal drugs and money from dealers. "And why not?" they would justify, like Jack's first partner Kyle Richards, who justified taking bribes to overlook traffic offenses. Officers Allen Mitchell, Scott Hill, and Terrance Carter were caught in a sting operation that was initiated following drug dealers' brazen complaints that officers were ripping them off, putting a serious strain on their drug-trafficking business.

The arrested officers began their activities against drug dealers by sifting some of the confiscated money and drugs from their arrests, giving operational money and drugs to other dealers who were their cooperating informants—a common practice that allowed officers to go after the bigger drug-dealing enterprisers. Their scheme broadened for them to take all the drugs and money from dealers without making an arrest and without saving the money and drugs for use to motivate cooperating informants.

The officers instead became dealers themselves, selling their confiscated drugs and living large on the stolen money. They justified their criminal scheme by saying they were denying street dealers their continuing dealing opportunities. The police were cleaning up random street deals that could create more users, while they themselves could sell the drugs only to addicted junkies, they claimed, who would never be rehabilitated anyway. There is always an argument to justify anything.

There were other cases of police and other government corruption—too many for Keegan to readily recall—but he knew that to ferret out any corruption, all you need to do is follow the money. Any unusual deposits, transfers, or spending will bring you to the doorstep of corrupt activity. One's income is usually regular and predictable, and things acquired are predictably within the value of that income.

Jack Keegan would come to know that there is no place more corrupt, in all levels of government, than Mexico and the other South American countries. Drug-trafficking cartels rule those countries and are moving steadily and quickly into the United States to flood political influencers with lots of cash—more cash than even big corporations can provide—to get their way in governance. Keegan wanted to help fight in the war on drugs, even knowing that it would be a losing battle.

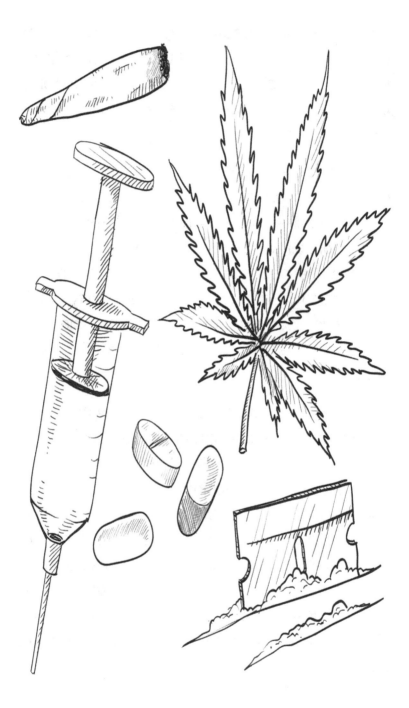

Chapter 6

The Drug Wars

It was thought by most to be a mistake that Jack took a requested next assignment to the Narcotics Unit of the Vice Control Division, where he hoped to make a big difference in fighting crime. He expected to and did get a lot of "action." Family and friends thought Jack was "*oobatz*," but he tackled the job. He also started law school, where he studied the general curriculum but concentrated his attention on criminal law.

Keegan and others in the class asked his criminal law professor who specialized in criminal defense in his private law practice,

"How could you defend scumbags for a living? Is it personally rewarding to allow so many to go back on the streets?"

"You are learning to be attorneys," the professor answered. "Remember that when you serve your clients you are serving social propriety and order.

You are there to assure that the law is fair to all without any abuse of power and authority. It is how it works!"

Jack Keegan never forgot his professor's answer and would see firsthand what it meant. He went on to become a "narc."

Keegan first had to learn the drugs—by pharmaceutical and street names and by weight (by grams, ounces, pounds, and kilos). He had to learn packaging and street values. He had to learn the acceptable street language of using and dealing drugs.

Jack had then to learn the hierarchy of known drug-dealing gangs and their territories. He was not to hit the street to fight drug trafficking until he knew everything about the nefarious trade. Only then could he develop and interact with confidential informants or assume an undercover role in an investigation.

Jack's father, however, expressed his displeasure with undercover sting operations; he did not approve of any officer who would gain the trust of a person through deception to make an arrest. He honored loyalty to be a virtue, even among thieves, and believed the police should not stoop to a lower level. But he knew it had to be done sometimes to uncover serious criminal activity. Nevertheless, he saw deception to be a personal character flaw.

Jack knew he was not well suited for undercover assignments anyway. His all-American looks would give him away. There were real junkies out there that were more suited for undercover work—for a price. Junkies and dealers were always open for personally rewarding business deals. Narcotics agents had to provide money and drugs to informants to support their habit, and even their business, in exchange for their cooperation. It was the only way they could get to the high-level dealers.

The Narcotics Unit of the Vice Control Division introduced Jack to the drug enterprises that would later so handsomely reward his law practice. Jack Keegan got to know all the players that would someday be his clients. But he had to do a lot to gain dealers' trust to protect them while targeting others. It was a shell game.

It was also a no-brainer, however, if people got killed. Offenders in drive-by shootings or assassins were never given breaks to be snitches, nor did they expect that they would be. There was no upping the ante that would make murder tolerable. No one could be treated worse than a killer. And if you killed or tried to kill a policeman, even if you were unaware that he was a policeman, you were dead in the water. Police killers were shown no mercy by any law-enforcement officers, not even by the FBI.

All too many times, Keegan recalled police officers who were gunned down unexpectedly. His close friend, Mark Hagen, became one of them. It was a cold winter evening in late February when Jack Keegan responded to a call to see his friend and police academy classmate one last time. A call to the Ravens Pub at the corner of Foster Avenue and Ravenswood brought Jack to see his childhood and police academy friend Mark Hagen's lifeless body along with Hagen's partner, Robert Traceras, lying in pools of blood on the barroom floor.

Mark Hagen and Robert Traceras were assigned to the Task Force and proudly wore their "TF" patch on their shoulders. People would call the unit "Tough Fuckers," causing the unit to be renamed "Special Operations Group," with "SOG" and then "SOS" (Special Operational Services) to replace the "TF" patch. The aggressive unit was since disbanded.

That night Hagen and Traceras noticed a suspicious man leaving the bar only to step back from his car and run back into the bar. He had a brown paper bag and was a suspected junkie. He didn't even wait to be approached. Hagen and Traceras were shot three times each without returning fire. Police officers responded from all over. Officers were approved to work overtime to help catch their killer. All other calls were put on hold.

Mark Hagen's and Robert Traceras's bodies were brought to the hospital for pronouncement and preliminary examination. Jack went there to see his friends' lifeless bodies. Remembering Hagen's permanent smile and impeccable grooming, Jack could not even recognize Mark. His expressionless face of death and still-open eyes with a dark blank stare jolted and enraged Jack and all officers crowding the emergency room. There would be hell to pay for this, and swiftly. They all knew that the killer would not be taken alive. It was time to find him.

The top-brass command personnel were all at the crime scene, directing all assigned and volunteer units where to search. They soon learned the killer's identity and all known associates and hangouts. Their search took them to a Wisconsin house where he was known to frequent. The FBI got involved being that there was interstate flight. Local police used "hot pursuit" as reasoning to leave the state. Everyone wanted a piece of the running "dead man." And they all shared the kill.

The killer's suspected shelter was surrounded. A weak shout-out for him to surrender was barely heard before doors were flung open and bullets were flying. The FBI took their shots as well. One agent was injured, being shot in the leg. Two police officers were also shot, but they recovered. When it was over, a pathetic pile of mangled, bloody flesh was all that was left of the drug-dealing junkie killer, who will remain nameless so as not to dignify his existence.

Keegan was still feeling the anger that overcame him when his friends were killed so many years ago, that they were denied the long lives that were expected of young men. He thinks of them often, as he continues to enjoy his life, wondering of all the life experiences that those killed were denied.

Jack also remembered that not long after, there was another friend who went deep undercover and was setting up a drug deal. His name was Doug Mayweather, a narcotics agent with MEG (Metropolitan Enforcement Group). The deal went bad in minutes. While sitting in the front seat, Doug invited the purchaser of staged drugs into the back seat.

"You got the money, Teak?" Doug asked while turning to Teak Jackson.

"Sure," Teak nodded and reached into a bag.

"Will this do?" while pulling an automatic pistol from the bag and firing it at the side of Doug's head, fully expecting to keep his money and steal the drugs.

Teak's gun misfired! A dud cartridge suspended animation for seconds until Doug was able to re-gain enough composure to return fire, killing Teak. Talk about a near-death experience! Doug counted his blessings and soon transferred out of his unit to more predictable, safer duties. No one could blame him.

But even those often-told experiences did not change Jack's direction. He had little fear of the gangs that protected their drug dealers. After all, his CPD gang was more than 13,000 strong with more available resources. And in those old days, the bad guys feared the police. It motivated each officer that the others would have their backs. There would always be swift retribution to avenge a fellow cop. Street justice—it is how things worked.

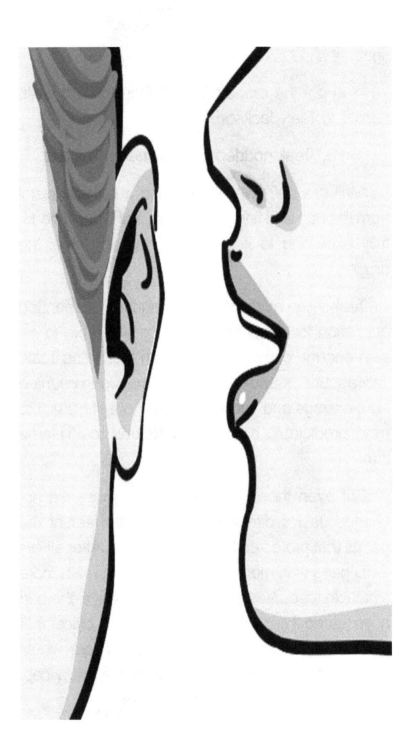

Chapter 7

Cultivating
Informants

Keegan began cultivating drug users and dealers to get the top guys in charge. Raphael Martinez would become one of those cultivated dealers.

Raphael was a low-level dealer when Jack first met him. He had been arrested several times before and did his time without giving up others in his trade. It was his silence that would allow him to move up in the drug-dealing hierarchy. But Jack was smooth in cultivating him to be a snitch. His drug-enforcement unit gave Jack a lot of tools.

It was chilly but not too cold when Raphael was observed huddling in a hallway outside what was suspected to be a drug house. Jack and his team broke up a suspected transaction between Raphael and a drug purchaser.

"Freeze, with your hands in the air where I can see them!" Jack commanded. A bag of money and drugs fell to the ground, and Raphael was unable to reenter the bolted steel door to the drug house.

"What do we have here?" Jack questioned. In typical fashion, Raphael said nothing. The unit team effected the arrest and took Raphael in for interrogation. That's where Jack put on the squeeze.

"You're a three-time loser already, Mr. Martinez," Jack said, giving Raphael some minimal respect.

"It is suggested that you work with us if you want to see the light of day again. We can play it like this case never even happened," said Jack.

"What do I have to do?" Raphael said, resigned to cooperate if the terms were right.

"Give us everything you know," said Jack, "and we will subsidize your operations with cash and drugs until your bosses are history. We want them, not you, unless you move up to assume their positions. Then you are fair game. Help us and stay relatively clean, and all of this goes away."

Raphael became a cooperating informant for Jack Keegan—a mutually rewarding relationship for years to come. Raphael knew that he could still make a handsome living while working with Jack's drug unit.

Drug-trafficking enforcement is the most dangerous of all police activity. Cartels distribute to transporters who supply dealers who supply users. All those groups will kill anyone in their way, and torture to death any who betray them, even undercover cops. It is a ruthless, dirty business. It takes ruthless and sometimes dirty enforcement techniques to make a bust. And when things look probable that a real bad guy will escape prosecution or not receive appropriate punishment, police have been known to make things right. It is sometimes the only way the police can gain some competitive respect—through fear of retribution, what the police refer to as "street justice."

Raphael Martinez was groomed, as were other informants, individually and unknown to the others, setting the stage to bust targeted drug suppliers. Officer Jack Keegan gave them their marching orders and would reward them if they were successful in their missions. Jack instructed them individually:

"You will wear a wire and report back with the identities and activities of all captured conversations you have with your suppliers. You will be doing that repeatedly until we are ready to make our move."

"What about my perks?" Raphael asked.

"You will get cash and drugs as you may need them to accomplish our mission," Jack said. "Check in periodically to let us know what you need."

Some drug unit informants didn't make it through missions. Some were caught by their targets and suffered ruthlessly to their death. Others ended up strung out on their own supply and fell short, helpless to function at all, much less accomplish their mission.

Jack Keegan's Chicago Police Narcotics Division work did not go unnoticed by federal drug-enforcement agencies. The DEA offered continued assistance if anything should involve upper echelon cartel trafficking.

It was spring 1977. One of Jack's informants notified him of a cartel soldier close to Guillermo "Memo" Echevarria, the cartel boss operating along the Gulf of Northern Mexico. He made frequent trips to the United States from Mexico on business. Keegan acted on the information and discovered the soldier was trying to undercut his boss by setting up his own trafficking deals. His name was Elijah Rico, a bodyguard and enforcer for Guillermo "Memo" Echevarria, a top drug lord and desired target.

Threatening to expose Elijah Rico, Keegan enlisted Rico's help. He would wear a device to capture whatever incriminating evidence he could obtain to target Echevarria. It did not matter that Rico would be back in Mexico to capture recordings. Rico knew that if he didn't comply, Keegan would expose Rico's betrayal of Echevarria.

But Elijah Rico came through. He had captured an incriminating conversation with Maria Vasquez, sister of Chicago native Vincent Vasquez, who would later survive an assassination attempt by Raphael Martinez. Maria Vasquez was the live-in girlfriend of Guillermo "Memo" Echevarria. She was also Elijah Rico's lover.

In her conversation with Rico, Maria Vasquez expressed her love to Elijah and that she would do anything to get away from Echevarria. He expressed his reciprocal love for her and his plan to branch off as a drug-dealing competitor.

Elijah Rico was a tall and handsome lover to

Maria, who was as elegant and charming as she was beautiful. They would have made an enviable couple had they not been caught up so deep into underworld activities.

Elijah initiated the recorded conversation with Maria during passionate lovemaking in his room: "I can't take this anymore, Maria; we must get away from here."

"I love you, Elijah; I love you so much!" Maria exclaimed. "Take me away from this pig. Let's start a new life together. We can do this," she said.

"Will you help me branch off into my own operation? We can do this together if you help me."

"I will! I will do anything for you, my darling."

Elijah Rico was assigned by Echevarria to accompany Maria on her frequent visits to see family in the United States. She was in Chicago when Keegan detained them both for an interview. Elijah's recordings of their intimate conversations were revealed to Maria for the first time.

Maria would, surprisingly, maintain her love for Elijah after learning that he recorded conversations with her that were turned over to Keegan. She wanted to be with him at any cost and did not want to be spared from any compromising position that he found himself in. Maria Vasquez was to be cultivated by Keegan to inform against Echevarria.

———∿∿———

The DEA was notified and set up a mission that would include Keegan. It would be a very dangerous proposition for Maria Vasquez to cooperate with law enforcement, but it would be equally dangerous to her lover, Elijah Rico, if Maria's recorded conversation were revealed to Echevarria.

"Ms. Vasquez, it is very important that you understand the seriousness of your situation," Jack Keegan emphasized.

"We are not in Mexico, but not very far from it either. The Echevarria cartel has enormous power to reach across borders to silence would-be witnesses against their drug operations.

"We captured your and other conversations that implicate the cartel in serious crimes enforceable in the United States. You need our protection. We need your cooperation. Work with us to bring them down. We will protect you and give you a new identity."

"What do you want me to do?" Maria

begrudgingly agreed.

Keegan gave Maria her assignment:

- "We need trafficking information.

- When and where will product deliveries be made?

- What are the routes and times of travel?

- Quantities.

- Locations of manufacturing.

- Names of people and organizations sending and receiving the product.

- Everything you can get."

Keegan went on to advise Maria Vasquez that she would not be wearing a wire. His team would confirm her information through other sources so as not to expose her cooperation. Being Echevarria's lover and mother to his young son, Maria's body would be exposed continually and probed by Echevarria. A bodily listening device could never stay concealed.

Having secured Maria's cooperation, Keegan with the DEA had to scramble to put an effective team together. He knew that drugs were coming to Chicago through multiple ports of entry. Jack would enlist the assistance of the DEA and of other states and municipalities adjacent to suspected drug-smuggling borders and ports. The DEA was on board, with Jack Keegan remaining exclusively in charge of all communication with his informant, Maria Vasquez.

"Don't even consider putting me at the scene of any arrest," Maria warned. "His men will know when I don't get pulled in with them—even if you try to fake my arrest, I will be dead. Memo will know. He will kill me if he even suspects I had something to do with it. Please," Maria pleaded.

Jack reassured her, "You must know that we will protect you, if for no other reason than because we need you to put him away forever. Don't worry."

It may have reassured Maria, but Jack Keegan knew how things go in these cases. Once Guillermo Echevarria was arrested, he had to be convicted, and her testimony would likely be required. It would be a challenge just to keep her cooperation from defense attorneys during trial discovery.

Jack felt sorry for Maria, but he needed her to make his case. It was his job to get Echevarria behind bars, and nothing would stop him.

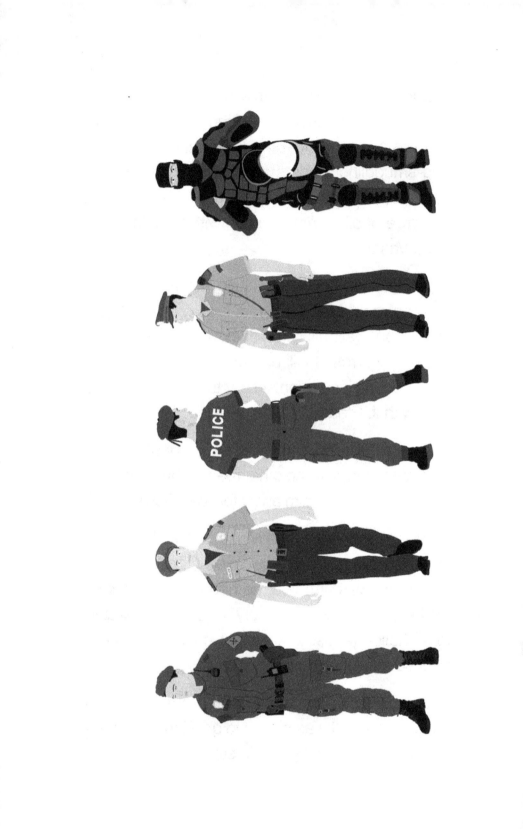

Chapter 8

Working with the DEA

It was hot—not just uncomfortably hot, unbearable. Nights in Mexico can be humid, but this night Elijah and Maria could almost see steam rising from their bodies. They'd just finished making passionate love. Neither of them could catch a breath of air as they gasped with their hearts racing. Their excitement was heightened by their fear of being caught. Guillermo Echevarria was down the hall in his home office doing some bookkeeping.

They whispered their plans for the week that would include being together but with Echevarria close by. There would be major movement in their product supply chain. Details were sparse but obtainable. Maria made her move.

"Good morning, Memo," Maria expressed to her fiancé. "You were up late last night; were you working hard?"

"Good morning, baby. I was trying to work things out to get product to Miami. Logistics have been tight lately," Memo replied. "Did you sleep well?"

"Never better. I'll be going to town later; need anything?"

"Not a thing, baby; I'm good."

Maria knew there would be plans, probably in cryptic code of some sort, lying around on his desk. She would gather anything she could for later perusal. She would take pictures of the clutter that she would leave undisturbed. Maria then left for town.

The pictures were quickly transferred to Keegan and deleted. She was unaware that the deciphered plans were of a major delivery from Mexico to Miami. Jack's team got together to plan their strike. It would take down the Echevarria cartel.

Echevarria's cartel soldiers were everywhere, but Jack Keegan was familiar with only those who operated in Chicago. The DEA filled him in on the others in Miami and elsewhere. To his surprise, some of his Chicago informants were also working in Miami. Jack reached out to broaden his grasp on them to enlist their cooperation.

It was different this time. Informants were asked to provide information that would close down cartel operations, not just a few competitive local dealers. It would be far more dangerous and certainly dry up business for a while. Jack and the DEA put on the squeeze.

Ruben Castro, Manuel Lopez, and Elrod Moses, all Keegan informants, were prepped and put in place for the sting. Keegan had never experienced such a sophisticated operation. It would reveal logistics that would give him keen insight to be applied in his later-to-be-developed criminal law practice.

Ruben Castro was arrested several times by Keegan. He was not initially cooperative and was difficult for Keegan to cultivate. Things changed after his third arrest. Castro saw that his cooperation could be personally rewarding to his trafficking business and was ready to flip.

Castro was always in Chicago but was known to travel occasionally to San Fernando and Quintana, areas some good distance apart along the Gulf of Mexico. He would be making those trips again for Jack Keegan and the DEA.

Ruben Castro was an unassuming, generally reliable, and likable scruffy guy that was accepted by the likes of Echevarria and other ruthless drug lords. He'd make his deals and get out, leaving plenty of profit on the table for everyone. He was good at his job.

Manuel Lopez and Elrod Moses each had their own sources but were both known to have similar cartel contacts in Mexico along and around the Gulf. They were not known to travel outside Chicago except occasionally to visit friends and relatives in Miami, Florida. They likewise saw an opportunity to expand their businesses. They were ready to help.

Raphael Martinez was firmly based in Chicago throughout his drug-dealing career. It was initially thought that he would be used only as a consultant this time to corroborate transport logistics learned by Keegan. He had valuable knowledge, however, about regular drug recipients at the various Miami ports of entry. After the sting operation began, he would be sent to Miami for the pickup.

Unlike with Maria Vasquez, all other informants would be wearing a recording device during all personal contact conversations. All phone conversations would be recorded and later deciphered when message specifics were vague or coded. All were to be transmitted as soon as possible through satellite telephone encryption.

The Department of Defense would provide the mission with two Blackhawk modified stealth helicopters to allow undetected strategic access to vulnerable cartel territories where rival cartel skirmishes could be incited.

Jack Keegan learned that there were many, many cartels operating throughout Mexico and South America. They were certainly competitive for business, but Jack understood that the cartels acknowledged the boundaries in each of their respective territories. It stood to reason that they could not conduct business if they were always doing battle with each other. Their operations were territorial, modeled after crime syndicates of Europe and the United States.

(U) Map 1. Mexican Cartels: Areas of Dominant Influence and Key Areas of Conflict

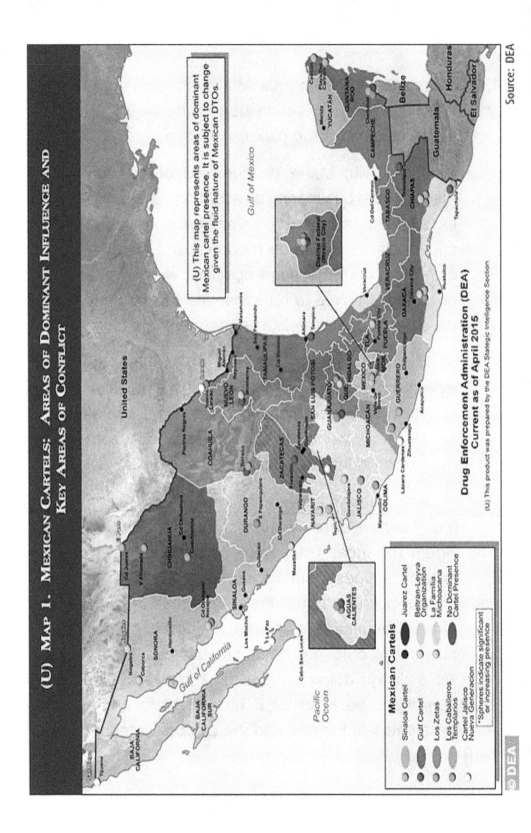

Source: DEA

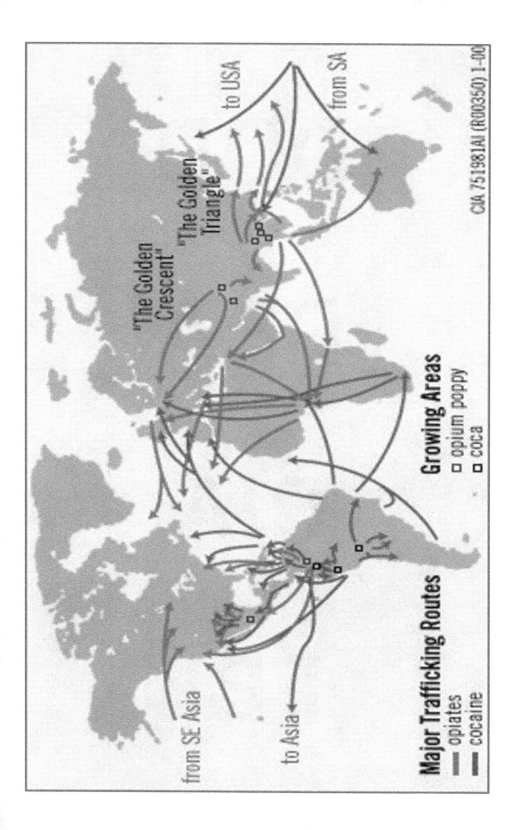

Major Trafficking Routes
— opiates
— cocaine

Growing Areas
□ opium poppy
□ coca

"The Golden Crescent"

"The Golden Triangle"

to USA

from SA

from SE Asia

to Asia

CIA 751981AI (R00350) 1-00

DOD

DEA

CIA

FBI

Chapter 9

Taking on Cartels

At the direction of the U.S. Department of Defense, a team was assembled to infiltrate cartels—a team of mostly DEA agents, Hispanic informants, and a few local narcotics cops who were close to cultivated informants. Jack Keegan was one of the locals responsible for Raphael Martinez, Ruben Castro, Manuel Lopez, and Elrod Moses. But Keegan's main contribution to the group was Elijah Rico, who brought Maria Vasquez to the table. Without Keegan bringing Rico, there would be no mission.

The DEA agents who set up the mission and provided Keegan with valuable cartel operational insight were mostly Hispanic, unlike Keegan and a few others who were not ethnically suited to infiltrate cartel operations, if necessary. The point DEA agent in charge of the mission was Ariana De Leon.

Ariana De Leon was a tough cookie. She was raised in New York, in the Bronx. An only child, she played with toy soldiers as a kid, never with dolls. Ariana grew up a tomboy with an interest in being a survivalist, eating bugs and things of the earth, if necessary, but prepared for any adversity that might come her way. She was always older and wiser for her years. She grew up with a fascination for studying historical battles of wars. Even her family was cautiously guarded against who she might become. But she was rational and well-focused in all that she undertook. Ariana was strong but sensitive to what was right and what was wrong. She was a true leader, well suited for her position on the mission team.

Ariana De Leon stood at an assembly room podium to address the team. The assembly room was a windowless paneled room with twenty or so folding chairs facing the podium. It was small for its purpose but would have been more suitable as a boardroom if instead furnished with a large table to seat the twenty. It would have been more comfortable and with the agents feeling more dignified and valuable to the gathering, but rickety cheap chairs and a wobbly podium would do. Typical GI furnishings.

"Good morning, fellow agents, and officers. We will begin our mission soon. All assets must be in place and ready. As you may know, we will be crossing the border near Laredo and moving southeast through Matamoros, San Fernando, Altamira, Tampico, and Veracruz. Many of you will be traveling by vehicles. Some of you will be parachuted by stealth aircraft at night into place and later extracted. All logistical coordinates will come from encrypted satellite images and transmissions. The NSA will be gathering and transmitting that information. No Mexican police or federales will be assisting us. We can't trust them. They are all bought and paid for by the cartels."

She continued, "As you also may know, we have expanded our mission to include targeting operations not only of the Echevarria cartel, but also of the Mendez cartel and the small Gulf operations of the major Mexican west coast Reyes cartel. We are not bringing military; we are seeding cartel competition to incite war with each other. Specifically, Echevarria and Mendez will squeeze Reyes out of the Gulf Coast and disrupt all operations enough to create a vacuum of leadership along the coastal area feeding Miami. We may have to move down farther to Yucatán if the major Perez cartel tries to take advantage of the leadership vacuum. For some of you, tasks may take longer to accomplish. Others will be extracted soon after placement. Before specific assignments, I will take questions.

"Agent Forrester?"

"How in hell will our team be expected to accomplish taking on four cartels?" Forrester asked.

"Not easily," explained De Leon. "We must disrupt all mentioned cartel operations to cause each to suspect the others of starting a territorial war. That is the mission objective. If a vacuum of territorial leadership is created, it may provide another opportunity for us to disrupt the major Perez cartel operations in Yucatán, along the U.S. border, and down the west coast of Mexico. This mission will begin a process that may slow the distribution of drugs to the United States."

The point DEA agent in charge, Ariana De Leon, was as beautiful as she was tough and fearless. She was only twenty-six, single, without family, not even her parents who'd tragically died in a car accident years ago, and dedicated to her job more than any other who Jack came to know in law enforcement. She was street smart and clever with an attractive and unassuming presence. She captured Jack's attention and his desire to know her better.

It was quiet in the assembly room following Agent Ariana De Leon's mission operational instructions to the group of agents and cops. As the group disassembled, and as De Leon still stood at the podium while shuffling papers, Jack struck up a conversation.

"Good morning, Agent De Leon; looking forward to working with you. If you have time, I would hope to have you explain how things work in your agency. I am unfamiliar with the obvious sophistication of your tactics. Maybe you have time now?

"Have you had coffee?"

"Love to," she responded, "I need my morning jolt of java."

As they adjourned to the cafeteria, Jack could not contain his attraction to her. He stumbled over his words that he worried would convince her that he was not well suited for the assignment.

"How long have you been doing this ... uh, a DEA agent? What's a pretty girl like you doing this for? I mean, do you like your job?"

"Hold on, pretty boy!" the agent exclaimed. "We're both here to do this job. Are you up for it?"

Jack composed himself, knowing that his approach used on one-night stands in Chicago would not work with De Leon.

"I'm sorry, Agent De Leon. I'm very sorry. You're just so beautiful."

"Let's start over, Officer Keegan. Thank you for the compliment, but let's start over."

De Leon went on to explain operations and her advancement in the DEA that brought her to lead the mission. Her beauty radiated as she spoke to Jack, sipping coffee and looking him straight into his eyes. She didn't lose her words or stumble. She was cool and collected. He continued to be mesmerized by a woman who had it all together. Jack would think it was love at first sight—for him at least. "Can we get to-gether later before we start our mission, Agent

De Leon?" Jack asked. "Maybe," she said, "but please call me Ariana. I'd love to see you later."

It was the next evening that the two would meet up for dinner and drinks and a later visit to Ariana's apartment. They would hit it off much better than at their first awkward cafeteria encounter.

Ariana took the lead again. She emerged from her bedroom and positioned her back to Jack. "Could you unzip me, please?" Ariana asked of Jack, who was again losing his composure.

She took no time letting her unzipped dress fall to the floor. She was naked and stunningly beautiful with a body hard and smooth as a mannequin, but angel soft. Her eyes were piercing with desire. She was ready for the best love-making Jack could ever experience. He knew it was good for her too, but Ariana was a woman of few words when it came to expressing feelings.

Exhausted with satisfaction, it was then time for sleep before Ariana's morning jog and review of her upcoming mission details. She would work and play on a tight schedule. Jack pulled himself out of Ariana's bed, also exhausted with satisfaction, but unlike Ariana, he was not so eager to tackle his busy day ahead.

Agents were gathered the next morning and divided into groups. Jack was one of two non-Hispanics in his group. The others were bilingual and could easily assimilate with native Mexicans. He was introduced. There were four group members of Mexican descent: Juan Martin Gutierrez, Alonso Garcia, Luciana Perez, and Ivan Moreno. Jack's non-Hispanic partner was to be Greg Forrester. All except Jack Keegan were DEA agents. The other police officer participants would not be joining Keegan in this mission. Jack Keegan had all the cooperating informants needed for this one.

Jack would be responsible for his cooperating assets whom he brought to the mission, including Raphael Martinez, Ruben Castro, Manuel Lopez, Elrod Moses, and most importantly Elijah Rico and Maria Vasquez, all primarily to disable the Guillermo "Memo" Echevarria cartel operating along the Gulf of Northern Mexico.

Martinez, Lopez, and Moses would remain Stateside in Miami to identify incoming product to Miami. Castro, and of course Rico and Vasquez, would be close to Echevarria in San Fernando when it all went down. All of Jack's group would be driven to their various strategic destinations. Each of the participants would be advised only of their own assignment so as not to endanger others if confronted by target interrogations.

The mission goals were haughty but achievable, Jack thought. It began. Elijah Rico and Maria Vasquez were already back with Memo Echevarria in San Fernando, Mexico. Ruben Castro was brought there to score a big drug purchase for transport to Miami. Martinez, Lopez, and Moses waited in Miami for transport receiving and distribution instructions. Others were put in places along the Gulf Coast as far down as Veracruz and standing by for expansion to the Yucatán Peninsula.

Greg Forrester coordinated all transportation logistics and radio communication transmissions. He was more nerdy than rugged, but he was most critical to smooth operations.

Jack Keegan was traveling to Altamira near Tampico by Hummer with Ariana De Leon and Greg Forrester when intercepted by a lone state police officer on patrol. It appeared that the encounter disturbed the officer more than the agents, who figured he was up to no good and would not report the encounter. It would not be uncommon to see American agents in Mexican territory. Nothing would come of it.

When they arrived in Altamira, they checked into two rooms on separate floors at the City Express Hotel. Encrypted messages assured all was in place and going well.

Agent De Leon didn't waste any time setting up communication gear and satellite image transmission screens. As a backup, duplicate equipment was set up in their separate room two floors down. Housekeeping was declined, and "Do Not Disturb" signs were placed on the doors. Agent Forrester occupied the lower room, and Ariana and Jack shared the higher floor room. It was an opportunity for Jack that would not be realized being that Ariana was all business. She would never mix business with pleasure.

When things started to happen, it was pure mayhem. The night skies lit up like a war zone. Echevarria called for his lieutenant, Elijah Rico, to stand close. All cartel players were trying to discover who was causing all the commotion.

Each knew it was not started by them. Business continued during the mayhem. Ruben Castro was ready to place a purchase order large enough to require Echevarria himself to sign off. Castro approached the cartel compound gates. He was known by the security crew.

"Hey, Ruben. Wass up?"

"Here for a special delivery. Let me in to see the man."

"I'll let him know; hold on."

Elijah Rico took the message and said to send him up. Echevarria looked up from his desk at Ruben.

"What can I do for you, my Chicago friend?"

"I have a serious buyer and need a lot of product. I know you would need to approve the purchase. So here I am. I can give you details directly if you like."

"It's always good to see you, my friend. I know I can always trust any deal you bring to me. You'll have what you need. You can give details to Elijah. I'll sign off on it. Have a safe trip home. There is a lot going on in the city from the sound of it."

Elijah took the order that he knew would be reported back to mission agents. It would require two shipments by boats with hollowed compartments, purportedly sent separately to different Florida ports to minimize a major loss if one should be intercepted by authorities. Martinez, Ruben, and Moses were alerted to get ready to accept those shipments that were to be seized by DEA agents standing by.

The mission was also preparing to "stumble" upon the many other watercraft operating to transport drugs from South American and Mexican cartels to the seemingly wide-open Florida coastal areas. They would be looking for crudely but effectively made submarines that were designed to navigate to their destinations by periscope. They would be noticing unusually excessive outboard motors on small boats—one captured had twelve—that were designed to outrun the Coast Guard. They were preparing to disrupt cartel operations as much as possible during the incited cartel warfare—without leaving a footprint.

The mission was an unrecoverable hit to Echevarria, especially considering the upcoming siege by the Mendez cartel, who took the offensive believing Echevarria was trying to take over Tampico operations and then move on through Veracruz. The mission was working but not without unintended consequences.

Elijah Rico and Maria Vasquez were each packing belongings when surprisingly confronted by Echevarria.

"What's going on here? Where are you two going? Why are things in turmoil around here?" Memo asked. "I'm seeing gunfire flashes all around us here. Who's doing this?"

Elijah answered for both. "We heard things happening and want to get ready if we have to go, Memo," said Elijah.

"Why would we have to go? Where are my guards? Where are you both going?" said Memo.

"Come with us, Memo," said Elijah. "We must take the tunnels away from here until things die down."

"I don't like this, but let's go. We'll sort it out later," said Memo.

Echevarria, Rico, and Maria Vasquez fled through the tunnels with a couple of servants who carried Memo's scant belongings. They would come to the last tunnel's end at Matamoros, but across the U.S. border not too far from Laredo.

They were there met by the DEA and taken into custody without incident. It became apparent to Memo that he was betrayed. He turned to Elijah and Maria.

"Both of you? Et tu, Brute?" Memo asked in disgust, referencing Caesar's betrayal by the Senators of Rome, where Brutus was his closest aide.

Echevarria was held in custody as a "John Doe" until all agents were extracted and the dust settled, so to speak.

Elijah and Maria were in protective custody until debriefing and their testimony could be elicited for Echevarria's trial.

Echevarria was paraded across international television as a major catch by the United States Department of Defense. He was also seen by competing cartels to have initiated the drug wars that were being fought on the Gulf.

U.S. marshals assigned to secure the defendant and protect the witnesses dropped the ball and were not as discreet and careful as one would expect them to be with high-security detainees. The celebrity defendant, Echevarria, somehow escaped, and the witnesses, Elijah and Maria, were kidnapped while in protective custody and brought back to Mexico.

The drugs Ruben Castro ordered to be delivered were intercepted at the two Florida ports as scheduled by Rico. Manuel Lopez and Elrod Moses accepted delivery of 128 pounds of cocaine that was immediately confiscated at the Haulover Inlet near Miami, and the vessel was seized with four occupants. Raphael Martinez accepted with the Coast Guard 26.5 tons of cocaine in Port Everglades in Broward County with an estimated wholesale value of $715 million. Eight occupants were detained with the vessel. All drug dealers were slapping themselves for wasting what could have been a bounty that would have set them up for life.

Elijah Rico and Maria Vasquez were not heard from again but were said to be seen hanging by their ankles naked and headless from the Mexico side of the Pharr-Reynosa International Bridge near Mexican Highway 2 in Tamaulipas State, Mexico. They were taken there to hang as a message to the U.S. that borders would not protect American citizens. It was an "in your face" message to America.

Ruben Castro never made it back across the U.S. border before the Miami seizures of the cartel shipments. He was found with his throat slashed and his tongue pulled through his throat—a fear-inducing sight that was commonly referred to as a Columbian necktie, suitable for cartel snitches.

It was a shame that Elijah, Maria, and Ruben did not live to see Echevarria meet his defeat. The Mendez cartel swept through Echevarria's soldiers to take over operations. There was a lot of bloodshed, but they took their time dismembering Echevarria. Even before being dismembered, he seemed a lot smaller than his reputation. His body parts were sent across Mexico to others who would dare to initiate warfare. No one ever discovered that he didn't start it.

The Reyes cartel suffered a lot of disruption being caught in the crossfire of Echevarria and Mendez and moved all operations back to the west coast of Mexico. It was okay since Reyes had better product pipelines by land across the

U.S. border rather than the all-too-risky Gulf crossings. The Perez operations remained stable in Yucatán, where they stayed put so as not to weaken their Gulf and west coast operations. All seemed settled, and the mission was deemed a success. Agents would return home to fight another day. Martinez, Lopez, and Moses continued their imports throughout Miami, but now from the Mendez cartel, being that Echevarria personnel were defeated and replaced.

All in all, Ariana De Leon's mission was a success. She caused the DEA and the Defense Department to take notice of her most impressive planning and execution capabilities. She earned many promotions and became powerful in the DEA administration.

But Jack Keegan was maturing from his experience, or perhaps he was just aging. It was good to be back home. He'd had his fill of drug enforcement—a war he knew would never be won. He was really done altogether with being a cop or any part of law enforcement. Even Ariana was losing her romantic luster, but never his respect. It was time for Keegan to move on.

Chapter 10

Becoming a Lawyer

B eing a police officer was the best part of Jack's life education. It was real. It was how things worked. But he left the job to settle down and utilize his newly earned law degree. He got a job with a big bond drafting and litigation law firm, but he did not stay long. Civil law practice was not his style. He wanted to settle into a criminal law practice.

During Keegan's short stay at his very first job as a new civil lawyer, Jack got a call from an old friend who was facing criminal felony charges for snorting cocaine while sitting in his car. His friend did not at first see the uniformed police officer approach to notice him inhaling the substance from a spoon. Jack took the case, pro bono, to help his old friend.

Before the preliminary hearing's initial court date, Jack had subpoenaed and received the police reports and dispatcher radio tape of the stop and arrest. It was learned by Jack that the arresting officer who approached his friend was in uniform, but the arrest and reports were prepared by a plain-clothes tactical team who identified themselves to have observed the crime "on view" (personally seen). Jack understood that the beat car officer handed the incident over to the tactical unit, presumably because the patrol officer's shift was ending, and he didn't want to be stuck working overtime with the case. The dispatch recording verified Keegan's suspicion that revealed a call from an otherwise unidentified officer calling for a tac-team to his location.

The case was called and both sides answered, ready for a preliminary hearing. The case was passed for the defense to discuss procedural motions with the prosecutor. Keegan warned the prosecutor against proceeding in the case.

"Your officer is about to perjure himself, counsel," Jack told the seemingly indifferent prosecutor. "Here's the evidence."

After hearing evidence and about Jack's police background that led him to know and understand what happened, the prosecutor decided to drop the case. But it was a victory that had to be first approved by the judge before he would allow dismissal. They went to the judge's chambers to get approval of the dismissal.

"You're new around here," the judge said, initiating a query into Jack's background.

Jack Keegan had to explain not only the evidence that was uncovered but also how Jack knew to investigate and obtain it. They discussed Jack's police background and finished with small talk. The dismissal was approved, and the case was recalled to enter the dismissal on the record.

Jack's courtroom experience as a police officer and his keen common sense led him to understand the judge's unusual intervention in the case. The judge didn't want to lose an opportunity to receive a "benefit" from the dismissal. After all, isn't the judge's role to dismiss cases? No! But in his courtroom, it was only *HIS* authority to allow.

Jack Keegan left the high-salary firm to join the Cook County State's Attorney Office as an

Assistant State's Attorney (or Asst. D.A., as one is commonly and welcomely called), where he learned to prosecute criminal cases. It was a cut in pay, but personally rewarding. And it was what Jack knew and liked—criminal law.

An early litigation assignment was in traffic court, a dirty, rat-infested old building that today houses a premier restaurant. Minor traffic cases would move through the system without serious judicial attention. Many judges would dismiss all minor cases in a courtroom because it was too crowded to give any cases adequate attention. A general announcement dismissed all cases and police officer witnesses, thanking them for their inconvenience to attend. Some judges thought that was punishment enough for any minor transgression.

More serious traffic cases, such as DUIs and Driving with Suspended Licenses, were treated more seriously, unless defendants were represented by one of the regular traffic-court defense attorneys, sarcastically called the "miracle workers." Jack Keegan's first trial as a prosecutor was against a DUI defendant represented by a miracle worker. Following a short trial the presiding judge said in his ruling,

"I can't find your client 'not guilty,' counsel," the judge said to the familiar defense attorney. "It is this prosecutor's first trial. How disappointing it would be for him to lose his first trial.

"Guilty," pronounced the judge, "but I am suspending judgment and sentencing. Next case."

Although, in fact, the case was Jack's first trial as a litigant, it was not his first courtroom exposure to injustice and irregularities. As a police officer, Jack witnessed many defendants walk free for no apparently adequate legal reason—and others sent to the "slammer" when evidence was weak.

Jack Keegan was next assigned as an Asst. D.A. to a misdemeanor courtroom on an upper floor of the Chicago Police Headquarters, 1121 S. State Street. It was a high-volume courtroom with little time to prepare prosecutions of all defendants demanding trial. Prosecutors had to cut plea deals quickly and prepare witness testimony where no deal could be struck to get through the busy daily court calls. And the judge tolerated no nonsense. He was tough.

Defendants in all courtrooms passed through a metal-detector screening upon entering. There was a day that one defendant got stopped with a switchblade knife on him. It was confiscated and criminally chargeable. But that wouldn't happen immediately. The knife was given to the judge, who took his bench off the record and had the arrestee brought up before him. Judge Cantrell leaned across the bench and held the knife to the arrestee, who was not then too distant. The judge growled,

"I ought to strip your pants to your knees and show you what I can do with your knife, you stupid son of a bitch. I will show you if I ever see you in my courtroom again. I'll be waiting for you." I will keep this knife and do that to you if you ever come into my court again." There was dead silence in the courtroom, where only the squealing elevated commuter trains then passing could not be stilled. Judge Cantrell was respected but feared. Perhaps it was fear that brought respect.

The knife-possessing defendant's case was called to be reassigned to another court so he would never cross Judge Cantrell's path again.

That incident was not the only time Judge Cantrell would violate expected proper judicial demeanor. He was a drinker, sometimes even in chambers with court calls backed up and litigants impatiently waiting to be heard. On occasion, other judges—or ones appearing to be judges—would have to take over his court to finish the cases. It was hard to tell if the people taking over Cantrell's call were real judges or other people just joking around with Cantrell in chambers who donned his robe pretending to be judges when they emerged to take over the court call. Rulings were made in Cantrell's name and entered on the record as judicial determinations. It was a joke that was not so funny. Cantrell, lawyers, and other court personnel who disgraced their positions of trust were later prosecuted and stripped of their jobs and authority. They all went to jail.

Misdemeanor courtrooms back then operated at a cadence that did not allow sufficient time to ponder what was going on. Regular defense attorneys entered the courtroom, asked the clerk to see a file, filled out a paper to file their appearance, and handed the file back to the clerk. Usually, you would see the clerk reopen the file to check its contents and remove something from the file jacket before placing it on top of the files to be called. For reasons un-known to most, some of those files were shuffled, and continually reshuffled, to the pile's bottom, not to be called until the end of court proceed-ings. Some attorneys approaching the clerk to request that their case be called were met with blank stares that ignored their request. Others would have their case brought to the top to be called next. Clerks held the power to call cases to be heard when they saw fit to do so. Such small positions that clerks held were seen to be big business. Some lawyers who would not toler-ate the clerks' hustle would at times approach the presiding judge directly in open court, demand-ing that the judge intervene to have the lawyer's case called. Sometimes the judge would inter-vene, other times the judge would not.

There were prominent lawyers that entered courtrooms where the waters would part, so to speak. Clerks would go out of their way to find out what case they were appearing on and call it immediately. There was seemingly always something in it for them. Those lawyers would always be first in line for a case disposition.

Sometimes courts went to recess to allow pretrial conferences. Those conferences were held between defense and prosecutors alone, mostly, but occasionally with the judge in chambers when specifically requested. Judges would sometimes propose case resolutions that were unrealistically favorable to one side or the other. After plenty of small talk and joking, courts would resume at their normal cadence.

Many defendants would not retain private lawyers before court for their misdemeanor cases, believing that they would get a public defender if needed. But if they posted a cash bond, or if attorney "hustlers" could otherwise secure payment from those defendants when entering the courthouse, those attorneys would swiftly solicit and dispose of defendants' cases. The hustlers would scramble to file their appearances without examining the files, except to review a cash bond receipt that they would claim at the case disposition. The court clerks would not have to open the file jackets in those cases before placing the files on top of the pile to be called. The attorney case hustling was understood by all to move the court call along more efficiently, without the need to continue cases for defendants to get their own private attorneys. Misdemeanor and preliminary hearing courts were the daily "offices" of the hustlers. Hustling was their only practice of law. And the courts allowed it.

Courtroom hustlers were fixtures at the misdemeanor courtrooms. They served their purpose, and some of them amused personnel with their antics. Two such hustlers were regulars at Court Branch 29. They would position themselves to be the first to approach defendants coming into the courthouse. The competition for defendant business was so fierce that they would be seen scrambling against each other to reach the corner bus stop to secure clients before defendants even entered the courthouse. Business was good.

The hustlers would banter with each other and with others who would pause to engage in conversation.

There was Danny Roberts, a colorful character right out of 1920s fashion, with wide-lapeled, wide pinstriped suits and fresh carnation boutonnieres pinned daily to his left lapel. His once broken nose added to his tough-guy look of an old-time Mob enforcer.

He snarled ethnic insults directly to anyone, friend or foe. He had his way about him that amused more than insulted. He also was a friend to Jack Keegan, who then was a prosecutor in the courthouse where Danny hustled his way through his practice of law. Even Jack would not escape his heritage insults. The Irish, you see, were all "pig shitters" (whatever that meant), and all nationalities were beneath his own unidentified ethnicity.

Danny Roberts was an opinionated family man with two boys whom Danny raised with strong beliefs. He wouldn't own a television that he was sure would brainwash his kids with liberal ideas of racial equality and interracial dating and marriage. He mocked the television shows like *Sesame Street* for spewing such liberal propaganda. He laid down the conservative parenting rules that his boys had better follow. They did. He kept his wife barefoot and pregnant, cooking, cleaning, and tending to her wifely and motherly duties.

Roberts was happy with his hustling law practice and invited Jack Keegan to join him when Jack would later leave the prosecutors' office. The court branch belonged to Danny Roberts, Danny thought, and it was his to share if he chose. Jack appreciated it but declined the invitation, stating that he would be opening a full-service criminal law practice.

"What do you wanna be, a *real* lawyer?" Danny quipped.

"Yeah. That would be nice," Jack retorted.

"You're a sucker looking forward to all that overhead and mileage going from court to court. Good luck, Jack, doing it your way."

"Thanks, Danny. And thanks for the offer to join you."

Nate Tyson was the second and only other Branch 29 courtroom hustler who operated with impunity. He was tall and thin and always blowing his nose. He was rumored to be a drug abuser in his spare time and often played straight man to Roberts, absorbing most of the jokes and insults Roberts hurled his way. They worked competitively to score the most client bond refunds in each day, but they were seen by most to work as a team.

The judge presiding in that courtroom was

gruff but friendly. He was a fair judge and a good man but tolerated the hustling activities that were known to be unethical in the practice of law. Hustling helped cases move along and was seemingly not his concern.

Then there was "Jingles." Frank "Jingles" Bonfanti was a low-profile bagman who collected "rent" from the hustlers there and in all the other branch courts that operated similarly. He was known as "Jingles" because he jingled his pocket change as he entered each courthouse to signal hustlers that it was time to make their weekly payments for their hustling privileges.

Jingles was a Chicago policeman who was the cousin of the court District Presiding Judge James Bonfanti. It was Bonfanti who sent Jingles on all his missions to collect rent from the courtroom hustlers. Jingles wore a light jacket over his patrolman's blue uniform when making his collections. He was Judge Bonfanti's personal bagman who, being related and rewarded for his service, was sure never to complain or snitch.

"Oh shit, here comes Jingles," Roberts

told Tyson.

"I have to get out of sight. I don't have the money for this today," he said as he slipped into the washroom. "I didn't even get my bond refunds from cases closed last month. These clerks aren't doing their job."

Jingles caught up with Daniel Roberts and complained, "What do I have to do with you, Danny? Turn you upside down and shake the change out of your pockets? Let's go; pay up. I know it's been a good week for you," Jingles threatened.

Roberts reached into his pocket to give Jingles what little he had with him that day.

"I'll catch you next time," Danny promised, "if business picks up."

The operation was smooth and worked well. It rewarded all collectively to get through the overcrowded daily court calls efficiently. It got things done.

Even the Chicago Bar Association saw the benefits that hustling provided. It implemented a program assigning bar members daily to courtrooms for them to receive cases passed by judges where bond was posted by defendants or where they asked for a lawyer. Case bonds would be refunded to defense attorneys by judges' orders upon case dispositions, just as was done for the hustlers.

The CBA charged a fee for membership and for assigning members to the various courts to obtain and service clients. It was the same as hustling without the solicitation. The Chicago Bar Association, like all bar associations throughout the country, was established to serve citizens in legal matters where they could not afford large fees for private attorney representation. The CBA encouraged members to serve the public "pro bono" or for reduced fees in criminal cases, commonly by taking defendants' bond refunds. Like hustling, the program helped to move cases along and provide supplemental income to attorney members. Jack Keegan saw the program to be almost identical to hustling, although the Bar Association program was not seen to be racketeering.

Most prosecutors were unaware of the business arrangements that allowed hustling, but Jack Keegan had more street smarts than most prosecutors. He knew how things worked in the city that enjoyed the reputation of a well-oiled enterprise that had operated that way for generations. It seemed to Jack that everyone knew or should have known how things worked. Jack Keegan thought it was no big deal. The feds thought otherwise.

Unknown to everyone, the feds were running a sting operation named "Operation Greylord," referring to the powdered wigs worn by the British ruling lords of "King's Bench." The operation cleaned up alleged pervasive corruption throughout the courts in Cook County. Although the operation could have run in just about any county, Jack thought, Cook County took the hit, and a lot of good judges and lawyers were taken down.

Unexpected federal convictions for racketeering, conspiracy, bribery, tax evasion, and mail fraud followed. Federal prosecutors were testing the waters, so to speak, to see if they could successfully apply statutes that were used to prosecute crime syndicate defendants. It was learned that just about any business activity could be sullied to apply those statutes. Hell, it was learned that even a Christmas gift to your mailman could land you in jail.

Chapter 11

Justice from the Hip

There was a very fine judge, Robert Johnson, who Jack Keegan knew quite well who was caught up in the ongoing federal sting operation. It was learned that the government fabricated a misdemeanor retail theft case that was placed before that judge for adjudication. An undercover government lawyer posing as a defense attorney representing an agent posing as a first-offender defendant (one having no prior arrest) appeared before Judge Robert Johnson. The bogus defense attorney appeared before Judge Johnson and requested a conference with the judge for a proposed case disposition. Keegan was in the courtroom when the case was called.

"Sheet 1, Line 22, People v. Rachel Eisenberg," the clerk announced, calling the defendant to stand before the court.

"Here, Your Honor," the bogus defense attorney replied while bringing his bogus client to stand before Judge Johnson at the bench.

"We are asking the court to participate in a conference to see if we can dispose of this matter, Your Honor. It is a minor retail theft case."

"Have you spoken to the prosecutor for a resolution, counsel?" asked Judge Johnson.

"No, Your Honor, but we feel a more acceptable court disposition may be reached in conference with the court."

Jack Keegan heard the preliminary conversation at the bench, as he heard to be no different than any other case where a conference with the court was requested. He also heard the admonishments by the court advising the defendant that in conference the judge would hear evidence and arrest history of the defendant that he would otherwise be unable to know if the case were to go to trial. The defendant acknowledged and waived her privacy rights, and her case was passed for a conference as so many others were that day. There was nothing unusual afoot.

In conference, it was learned, Judge Johnson offered a disposition of non-reporting "court supervision"—an expungable non-conviction disposition that can be erased from one's arrest record if the supervision period is completed without further criminal activity. It was a disposition that was usual in minor cases where the defendant had no prior criminal record.

The State had no objection to the judge's proposed disposition and would have offered it to the defendant if only asked before the conference was held. Even a plea of guilty before any judge without a defense attorney and without a conference would have brought such a case to the same disposition.

Judge Robert Johnson was nevertheless indicted but acquitted by a reasonable jury that was made to understand the trumped-up charge that showed no improper influence motivating the proposed case disposition.

The power of the federal government to charge crimes where none existed did not escape Jack Keegan unnoticed. He felt that its power illustrated the importance to check and balance all authority to assure fairness. Even an acquittal can ruin one's reputation forever.

It is not to say that some judges and lawyers were not deserving of prosecutions. Many were. Here, there, and everywhere. But there was a lot of nit-picking during Operation Greylord to make it look like everyone was in cahoots to make money. It was an unjust smear campaign on Cook County generally, Jack Keegan thought. It was to reinforce the county's reputation for being "*Crook* County."

Jack Keegan believed that protocols should always be in place to provide checks on authority that would *prevent* even the appearance of impropriety. Authority should be checked continually to prevent abuse, rather than setting up stings to bring criminal prosecutions for abuse.

Nit-picking aside, Keegan instinctively knew that criminal judicial activity was afoot. Gratuities and bribes that may influence outcomes in serious criminal cases are repulsive to any system of justice, and there were some judges in some courts, and many lawyers, that could not be redeemed without prosecution.

Criminal court judges were and still are

randomly assigned before arraignment of the defendants. Newsworthy, high-profile cases, however, seemed to be specifically assigned to the same group of seasoned, well-qualified, and respected judges that would not embarrass the judiciary with questionable rulings. Occasionally a case would be assigned to another judge, randomly or upon a defense attorney's motion to substitute the judge in his client's case. It was in those cases that eyebrows would rise among attorneys who were familiar with corrupt tactics.

One such judge who received suspiciously assigned cases was Judge Ambrose Johansen. Jack appeared before Judge Johansen and was sometimes amused. Judge Johansen would emerge from his chambers to call cases for defendants that needed to be arraigned and those cases to be conferenced for disposition. Others would be called that were continued for sentencing after trial. One defendant being sentenced after previously being found guilty spoke after being sentenced to twenty years:

"Judge, please. I can't do that kind of time."

"Well, sir, do the best you can," Judge Johansen replied. "Take him away, Mr. Sheriff."

Judge Johansen struck fear into all defendants who stood before him. Even prosecutors and defense attorneys were afraid of his unpredictability—that is unless case outcomes were predetermined in conference. Jack Keegan approached the prosecutor in his client's case.

"Can we work this case out?" Jack asked Aaron Jenkins, the prosecutor in Jack's case.

"Ask the judge if he will conference it; all dispositions have to be offered by Judge Johansen," Jenkins replied.

Following arraignment, Jack's case was passed for a conference in chambers.

Jack Keegan was representing one of his former informants when he was a police officer, Elrod Moses. Moses was charged with possession and intent to deliver a large quantity of heroin laced with fentanyl. It was a super-X felony calling for a minimum nine-year penitentiary sentence. Keegan privately questioned Moses again before conferencing to review irregularities affecting his arrest:

"Where were you standing when the police approached you? And it was dark, right? A bag was passed to another who dropped it after the police lost sight of him, right? He got away. They put the bag on you, right? You never claimed it to be yours, right?"

"Yes, right to all questions," Moses replied.

No motions were yet filed before the conference. The judge liked lawyers to straight-shoot from the hip before any lawyerly procedures or arguments. He would let the lawyers pitch their version of their cases and size up a case quickly to offer his proposed disposition. Jack took his seat in the judge's chambers at court recess. The prosecutor took his.

"What do we have here?" asked Judge Johansen.

"People v. Moses, a super-x possession with intent; we would accept the minimum—nine years IDOC," said Aaron Jenkins.

"What do you say, Keegan? Will he take that?" Judge Johansen asked.

"Your Honor, I know this defendant from my years in CPD Narcotics. He was a very helpful informant. That aside, he was not in possession of the bag containing the drugs in this case. 'A bag' was reportedly found that was abandoned by another who ran away, although the police would say they never lost sight of the bag that, they would say, was originally held by my client, Mr. Moses."

"Any background, Mr. Jenkins?"

"No, Your Honor; none reported."

"Your client's case will be reduced to straight possession with a stipulation to a probational weight. Thirty months' probation with community service satisfied by his cooperation with the police in any ongoing investigations."

"Thank you, Your Honor. We will gladly accept your proposal," Keegan said while beginning to stand.

"Hold on, Judge," exclaimed Prosecutor Aaron Jenkins. "The State will not reduce this charge to allow probation."

"Very well then. You have your arresting officers here in court. Put your case on. I'll hear it today. Answer 'ready for trial,' counselors, and put it on," Judge Johansen said scoldingly to the prosecutor.

The two prosecutors in chambers whispered to each other, and Jenkins conceded,

"All right, Judge, we will reduce the charge for the disposition. We will agree."

They, of course, knew the judge was signaling that they would lose at trial if they did not comply.

Judge Ambrose Johansen took complete control of his court call. If he felt it appropriate to amend charges or even dismiss them, he would see to it that it was done. But it was a crapshoot if you had no mitigation. Defense attorneys were forced to recommend clients to take severe sentencing offers that if not accepted would bring much harsher sentencing after trial. It was effective.

Keegan thought that Judge Johansen's protocol for pretrial conferences left much opportunity for corruption, however. That much control over proceedings certainly could provide an appearance of impropriety, even when there was none. Judge Johansen was respected as being a tough but fair judge and was never challenged for his courtroom demeanor.

That was not the case in Judge Daniel Madden's court. Jack Keegan recalled his first appearance before Judge Madden.

"Call my 9:00 a.m. clients and have them wait for me. I have to get to an early arraignment with Judge Madden. I'll get to the others as soon as I can," Jack told his secretary, who coordinated Jack's court calendar and kept a lid on conflicts. She was always extending apologies for his late arrival to courts.

Jack ran up the stairs and crammed into an elevator at the Cook County George N. Leighton Criminal Court Building only to wait for the judge, who always started late. He didn't know that about Judge Madden until that day—a day that required his appearance in three other courtrooms at two other courthouses. He had to leave and told the judge.

"You can't leave counsel," Judge Madden warned.

Keegan waited until 11:00 a.m. for the judge to grace the court with his appearance. Jack's other cases were continued by the other courts. It would be the last time putting Judge Madden's court first on Jack's agenda. But that would be the least troublesome of Keegan's experiences with Madden. He was corrupt to the core.

Madden was a stout blustering Irish drunkard who thought all lawyers were earning more than he could as a judge. And why, he thought, should they deny him a piece of their action? It was soon learned that lawyers had to pay homage to him if you expected anything to go your way.

If you entered Judge Madden's chambers near Christmas, you would see bottle after bottle of liquor lined up on his credenza as if to announce his holiday gift preference. If you entered with your hands empty, you might be ignored—at least until he finished his joking with his circle of friends. And then you would need to state your purpose and leave until you understood the proper rules for entry.

Any casual introduction would prompt his inquiry about your case—not just about the substance of your case but also about your fees and expectations.

"You're Jack Keegan, aren't you?" Madden asked soon after their first meeting. "It's nice to see an Irishman here. We all have better common sense than most. What kind of case do you have, and what are you looking for?"

Warren J. Breslin

"I'm here on a drug case that was arraigned last week. I'm waiting for discovery to get a better handle on what I have," Jack replied, not ready to discuss anything about his case. Not only for that reason, but also there was no prosecutor present. It was to be an unethical *ex parte* communication that Jack tried to avoid.

"Who cares about evidentiary discovery, Jack?" Madden asked with a level of familiarity that he would express with a newfound friend.

"Tell me about your client. He can't be a strung-out user if he can afford *your* services. How much does he make? What is he expecting from you on this case?"

Jack Keegan's unanswering smile clued Madden that Jack was not going to "play ball." The conversation ended right there abruptly, and Jack excused himself from Madden's chambers. Judge Madden allowed Jack to have his case transferred with some lame motion scribbled by Keegan. He would forever file his motions to substitute judges in all future cases assigned to Madden.

Jack heard through the grapevine that Madden later dismissed a murder case where a

156

Mob hitman paid $25,000 to walk—a small price to pay to get away with murder.

Undercover federal agents got him in that case and other serious cases in which he sold his robe for cash. During the pendency of his case before trial, Madden was seen wandering the skid-row streets of Chicago, drunk and penniless. He got what he deserved, Jack thought: more years in the penitentiary than he had left to live.

The hitman who Judge Madden acquitted was retried and sentenced to death. There was no double-jeopardy defense being that he was never in jeopardy in the fixed case. The moratorium on the death penalty in Illinois converted his death sentence to life without parole. Jack recalled that he was still alive, doing his time.

Released after completing his sentence, Madden was found mumbling and pissing in his pants while sleeping under a viaduct in a cardboard box, a booze bottle still in hand.

Chapter 12

Gypsies: A Class of Their Own

Probably the most interesting group of clients a criminal defense attorney may be lucky enough to acquire is the group of various clans or tribes called "Roma." They even speak their own Romani language among themselves. We call them Gypsies if they are descendants of India or Travelers if they descended from England or Ireland. Whatever you may label them, they are a group unique and contrary to our civilized customs and traditions. They are thieves and don't deny it. They are even proud of it.

Gypsies traveled Europe from India as far back as the Middle Ages. They were called Gypsies because they were then thought to be Egyptians. Other names and labels put on them all referred to their main characteristic—that they were all itinerant wanderers and soothsayers.

Most criminal defense attorneys do not want to deal with "shifty" Gypsy clients. And most Gypsy tribes—or "nations" as they preferred—boasted of their own reliable lawyers. The tribes were territorial, and each tribe's personal lawyer contact information was sold to visiting out-of-state or out-of-territory tribe kings when requested. The Gypsy Kings, heads of each nation, had regular council meetings to determine their scamming agenda and prices to pay for their lawyer referral services, and other things, including sale prices for their daughters, who were for sale to other tribes' young men to solidify their territorial power.

Gypsy women set up shopfronts in their homes as fortune-tellers. A common practice even today, when customers appear gullible enough, is to gain the confidence of those customers so the fortune-teller may ward off all evil spirits that may be lurking in customers' lives. Hundreds of thousands of dollars have been scammed from people who brought and left their cash money to be "cleaned" of evil spirits with overnight candlelit vigilance of a container that encouraged those evil spirits to leave the physical money and never return. Of course, the customer returned the next day to find that the evil spirits took the cash with them when they left.

Gypsies will say various things to convince the patsy customer that it was an exceptional thing that the money was gone and that perhaps it will return if they wait a little longer. If the customer comes to realize the scam and calls the police, they are always laughed at, and usually the complaint is unfounded.

Jack Keegan represented Gypsies in many of those cases that went to court due to bank receipts verifying large cash withdrawals. Unfortunately for the complainants, Gypsies never gave receipts to hold the cash. The cases were generally dismissed as unbelievable or just unable to be proved. During the pendency of those cases in court, Keegan received too many calls from the Gypsy clients wanting to know what would happen in court. In frustration to answer the pesky clients, Jack responded, "Why don't you check your crystal ball and tell me?" He could never understand why his clients were never amused by his answer.

Gypsy men were always home-improvement contractors who drove through neighborhoods to offer their various services such as driveway and roof repair or even structural repair of brick or paneled siding. They often worked in pairs and suggested that they enter the prospective customer's home to examine home repair needs and prepare written estimates for the jobs. One of the pair would rifle through the homeowner's belongings while the other kept the homeowner occupied in another room.

When a homeowner allowed a Gypsy onto his roof for examination, the Gypsy would lean against a chimney after placing a strap around it and hold both strap ends before twisting the chimney, causing damage that would be found by that Gypsy to need repair. Those Gypsies were appropriately called "chimney shakers" and were regular criminal clients of Jack Keegan.

Another case that was disturbing, even to Jack who had seen it all, was a case where bank video evidence showed his Gypsy client hovering over a ninety-year-old woman while directing her to withdraw a significant amount of cash for a scam home repair. It was a case that Jack Keegan was glad to have lost, although he tried his best to win. In a way, he took his loss to be a win in that it better served justice. That same client bragged to Jack of his mother, who the Gypsy client claimed to be the best pickpocket and shoplifter who ever lived. The gleam in the Gypsy's eyes as he talked with pride about his thieving mother was disgusting. No wonder, Keegan thought, why so many lawyers would not take Gypsy cases.

Gypsies never sought to be documented, not even with birth certificates that none of them had. They were born with Gypsy midwives and always home schooled, which was no schooling at all. Most could not read or write. Amazingly they survived so persistently over centuries of antisocial behavior.

As illiterate and repulsive as they were, they took pride in having a good lawyer that would keep them out of jail so they could move on to other jurisdictions to sell their scams there. They would boast of their lawyers who some thought were too expensive. But high fees were gladly paid in cash up front. They felt wealthy and important. They wanted their lawyers to dress sharp and fly first class to distant court locations where legal services were often needed. They wanted their lawyers to be socially revered—a reverence that they could never themselves achieve.

Chapter 13

Joining the "Big Boys"

Although Jack Keegan's Chicago clientele brought the bread and butter to Jack's law practice, the big fees were earned in Miami through his former drug-dealing informants and other contacts he acquired during his years in the Chicago Police Department. They trusted Jack to be straight with them and do his best to win their cases. Sometimes they needed guarantees that Keegan knew he could never provide.

It was a different practice of criminal defense law in Miami. The usual one-man criminal law firms in Chicago were big five-to-thirty lawyers strong in Miami. Jack met with some attorneys there after admission to the Florida Bar and sitting in on court proceedings throughout the city to get a feel for the protocols. Jack found that no significant drug cases landed in state courts. They were all in federal courts. In fact, no minor cases ended up in any court, being resolved with mere citations—notices to pay fines by mail like treatment in Chicago traffic matters. Small quantities of drugs found by police were just confiscated with mere warnings to offenders. Business was booming for defense firms but with caveats from the regular attorneys practicing there.

"Get all fees up front and never give clients unrealistic expectations. You will end up in the canals," said Attorney Arthur Zimmerman, who warned Keegan about practicing criminal law in Miami. "And never meet up on a boat with anyone about business or with anyone who you don't know well. Lawyers have disappeared out there," said Zimmerman, pointing to the ocean.

Zimmerman seemed familiar with most of the "players" Jack knew, but his familiarity with cartels and their involvement with all aspects of drug transportation and distribution far exceeded Jack's. Zimmerman warned that cartels are always involved in the defense of their soldiers and will be the source of all legal fees. He emphasized that they need to get what they pay for.

Jack became close to Art Zimmerman and often went to him for advice. He had good knowledge about everything going on in Miami. Zimmerman had a special niche practice defending against government property forfeiture actions. A tour of nearby Key Biscayne, a wealthy suburb of Miami, revealed mansions plastered with forfeiture notices not to enter or trespass. Big cash money was spent to purchase and recover those properties. It was a revolving door of ownership, and it was always a confidential trust number that owned those properties.

Keegan learned that Miami was a cash city nurtured by drug cartels to serve their purpose. There are more banks flourishing in Miami than any other business. Miami is said to be the money-laundering capital of the world. Any taxi driver will tell you how productive and vibrant the city has become due to Cuban and South American migration. But who are those wealthy immigrants? Cartels.

A quick computer search would illustrate the pervasiveness of cartel operations throughout South America and their influence throughout the United States. Jack did his homework and knew who and what he would be dealing with. He also knew that he would be handsomely rewarded for his efforts. Keegan did his share to serve justice in a drug war that he knew would never be won by law enforcement.

It was late at Jack's new Miami office when a call came in from somewhere in South America. The caller spoke English but not too well.

"Jack Keegan?" the caller queried.

"It is," Jack responded. "What can I do for you?"

"We need a situation cleared up in South Florida. A friend was arrested and must be in federal court Tuesday. Can you help him? We heard you are the one to contact for this problem."

"I can meet with you tomorrow morning. What is your name and number, and who is the defendant?" Jack asked.

"My name is not important. Your client, Raphael Martinez, will see you at 9:00 a.m. with all information you need. Okay to see you then?"

"Okay, looking forward to it." Jack knew he would be taking a drug case involving his old informant when Jack was a cop. A new relationship would develop.

At 9:00 a.m. sharp, Martinez came into Keegan's office and dropped a pile of cash on Jack's desk.

"Good to see you, El," as Jack had learned to affectionately call Raphael. "What's your problem?"

"Your old friends at the DEA got me at the harbor in Key Biscayne with some product. I told my friends you were the one to call for help. I vouched for you, Jack. Don't let me down."

"You know how things can go in these cases, El. And they're a lot of work. Who is your backer here?" Keegan asked.

"I can't say that, Jack, but you know I'm good for whatever you need. Just give me a number; I'll get it," Raphael assured.

After learning the case particulars, Jack realized the value of his services and his likelihood of an acquittal. He dropped a number on Martinez, who did not flinch at the figure.

"I will need 250K in certified funds, but not cash."

"No problem, Jack," assured Raphael, knowing his backers would contact their bank to issue a clean check.

Jack would not prepare an Attorney-Client Representation Agreement that would include his inability to accept cash over $10,000 without reporting the payment to the IRS, and other conditions, that might spook the budding business relationship. He was playing with the "big boys" who knew how things had to be done. Likewise, the "big boys" would not express the possible negative consequences of losing their cases. There had to be mutual trust—with payment up front.

Jack Keegan had not yet counted the pile of cash Martinez dumped on Jack's desk, but he knew it would be short of his requested retainer. Keegan reached to count the pile.

"Don't worry about counting it. I'll tell them you need a quarter mil more. Just get me out of this," Raphael said like a big shot he never was before.

"Thanks, El. You know I'll do my best."

Keegan hurried to prepare for Raphael's Tuesday arraignment. He filed his appearance and preliminary motions and began preparing for his biggest case. It was a case he was compelled to win. There would be no alternative to an acquittal.

"May it please the court," Jack said in his introduction to the court, "my name is Jack Keegan, and I am asking leave to appear on behalf of the defendant, Raphael Martinez."

Judge Angus Baldwin was to preside over the serious, but relatively unnewsworthy, drug-trafficking case that was so common in federal court in the Southern District of Florida. There was not even a blink of an eye by any court personnel reviewing the charges that included large quantities of drugs being distributed in Miami.

"Very well. Mr. Keegan, we will give dates for the exchange of discovery material following arraignment. All preliminary motions must be filed shortly thereafter. We will set dates for those purposes," Judge Baldwin pronounced.

Volumes of materials poured into Jack's office following the arraignment. Keegan learned that Raphael's arrest was a result of a many-months-long sting operation that included many undercover informants. He knew the prosecutors would do everything to protect the identity of those informants. He also knew that their identities would be of major concern to the participating cartels. Vaguely worded and redacted police reports would be found throughout the discovery materials.

In a dilemma that concerned him on both sides of criminal proceedings, and even in grooming informants when he was a police officer, Jack Keegan knew very well what would happen to any informant identified, but he also knew that defendants have the constitutional right to confront witnesses against them. He struggled somewhat with the expectation that he would do everything to reveal identities, but in the end his job was to serve justice. The right to confront witnesses was more compelling to the defense—and to the cartels.

Jack met with Raphael. He discussed the evidence learned and those identified witnesses that surely would testify. Unknown informants that led to Raphael's arrest were discussed but left unidentified during the conversation. Jack would pursue their identities in court.

Keegan argued his filed Motion to Produce:

"Your Honor, Judge Baldwin, we ask the court to compel the prosecution to reveal the identities of certain individuals that may have necessary information for the defense and for the rebuttal of incriminating evidence expected to be introduced."

"The People object, Your Honor."

"We will hold an 'in camera' conference on this matter. In my chambers, counsels," Judge Baldwin ordered as he rose to lead counsels to his chambers.

"What do we have here, counsels? What is the relevance and sensitivity of the requested information?"

"It is imperative to the safety and further utility of our informants that their identities are not revealed," said the prosecuting Assistant United States Attorney (AUSA).

"But their information may be pivotal to our defense and the reliability of evidence. Mr.

Martinez needs to know the source of any evidence that will be used against him," Keegan argued. "You may be fishing, Mr. Keegan, but I will keep your request under advisement and order the prosecution to review and release any information that may lead to the defendant's exoneration if explored. The defendant is entitled to cross-examine any potential witnesses against him."

Keegan accepted the court's ruling that he knew would provide little information. He met with Raphael to discuss things that led to his arrest.

"Who do you suspect flipped on you, El?" Jack asked Raphael.

"I have an idea that I am exploring, Jack."

"Well, don't take too long. We need to prepare for the worst."

"I'll get back to you real soon," Raphael said confidently.

It was learned in the news that there was a common "drive-by" shooting in the Englewood neighborhood in Chicago. It was suspected by Jack to be local gang warfare until he heard that the killed victims were from Miami. Another gangbanger victim was found washed up on the pristine beach of Key Biscayne. Keegan suspected that El was cleaning up possible loose ends. He really didn't want to know.

Martinez showed up at Jack's Miami office to drop off the balance of his requested retainer. There was no discussion about the recent killings, and Keegan just talked about the case generally, with nothing urgent to be addressed. It was as if they communicated the witness issue resolution telepathically. Both were ready to proceed with confidence.

On the next court date, Judge Baldwin addressed counsels to approach the bench.

"An emergency motion was just filed in this case by the U.S. Attorney. It appears the U.S. is unable to proceed and needs more time to investigate evidence."

"On the record," Judge Baldwin announced as the attorneys moved back to their respective tables.

"The U.S. is moving to dismiss this case without prejudice and given leave to refile within their limited time should they desire. The Court will so allow. This cause is dismissed without prejudice on the Government's motion. Case dismissed."

Keegan whispered to Martinez not to gloat or show any emotion as the judge issued his order.

"Do not even make eye contact with the prosecutor. Just turn and walk out with me quietly. Do not talk with anyone about what may have led up to the dismissal. We are still way within the statute of limitations on prosecution. 'Without prejudice' means they will be allowed to refile your case within that time."

Martinez knew the drill and wanted to talk with Jack privately. He knew not to discuss anything by phone, so he wandered into Jack's office the next day.

"My man wants to talk with you privately. He has a yacht that you're invited to meet him on. He says tomorrow is good if you can."

"What does he want? Do you know?" Keegan asked.

"All is good; he just wants to thank you personally."

"No need," Jack quipped. "It's not over until the statute of limitations runs out. I have to be ready if the case comes back."

There would be no way that Keegan would ever agree to a meeting on a boat. He remembered quite well the warning notice given to him by his colleague, Art Zimmerman. No matter what the final outcome of any given case, a boat visit is potential suicide. Jack would never make himself so vulnerable.

"Never mind, then. I'll let him know what you said. He will wait for the final case disposition. Thanks again, Jack. You always have my back."

Keegan gave Zimmerman a call.

"All went well in my case, Art. So far, anyway. They may bring it back. You have a few minutes to meet up today?"

"Sure thing, Jack. Come on over. We'll have lunch," Zimmerman replied.

Keegan needed to explore all the dangers he faced in his newly enhanced criminal law practice. He couldn't be too cautious. They met at Art Zimmerman's office before heading out for an afternoon bite.

"What exactly will the cartels expect of me for the large money paid? Do I have to always look over my shoulder?" Jack asked.

"Everything, and yes you do! One thing you can rest easy about is money. Cartels don't look at your fees as a fixed outlay in cash. They see money as a cost of doing business and are okay with large legal fees if you can keep their soldiers working to make more than they lay out. They look to their cost efficiency—profit.

"Don't get greedy, and don't lose. You should be fine," Art continued.

"If you get lax, at least don't go near the water," Art said tactlessly with a smile.

The meeting with Zimmerman did not give the reassurance Jack hoped to get, but he knew that Zimmerman had been doing well in his practice for a long time. He kept telling himself all would be well.

As much as Art Zimmerman discussed proper protocol representing cartels, he distanced himself from Keegan during and after his cases—at least for a while after. He did not want to give advice in Jack's cases or even hear about them. Art advised that Jack would be on his own and wished him well. It unnerved Jack to feel the dangers of his more rewarding clientele.

Before long, word got out that Jack Keegan was the one to retain in big drug cases. Jack wouldn't even take on cases that were small. But small cases were few and far between in Miami. Even the police would not make arrests if the cases were too small. Every case was big. Every case was in federal court.

Jack got a call from his old acquaintance Elrod Moses, whom he knew as a cop, whom he groomed to be a confidential informant, and whom he successfully defended in Chicago criminal courts. Another anonymous call came in to arrange payment of legal fees to represent Moses, this time in a federal court in Miami. The charges were for drug trafficking and racketeering.

Elrod was already on bond when he walked into Jack's Miami office with a bag of cash. Jack knew that Elrod, as a soldiering comrade of Raphael Martinez, already knew the drill.

"I can't accept this, Elrod, without filing notice of cash payment over $10,000. I know that your bosses would not want that."

"Don't worry, Jack. This isn't a fee. It's a present for your birthday. I would have gotten something else, but I didn't have time to shop. We cool?"

"Okay, let's talk about what we have here. What happened?"

"I got sloppy, Jack. If I didn't learn from the street, I should have learned from you on our last dance in Miami and Mexico. I didn't know the guys I was dealing with. It was a second-hand introduction. My bad."

"Hand-to-hand delivery is tough, Moses. Was the delivery to the law or a citizen buyer?" Keegan asked.

"I think both. They set me up to make three deals at different times. There were different buyers with a different snitch each time."

"I will check out what they have on you. If they can make the case, I will see what they will do. We worked well together last time," Jack said to Moses. "Let me try to get more mileage out of your cooperation in that mission. They might want to keep a handle on you. I'll talk with the prosecutor before the court date and get back to you then."

Keegan thought about what he was getting into with Elrod Moses. He had previously groomed Elrod to be an informer when Keegan was a drug cop, and now he might offer him up to do it again against the very people who would be paying Jack's fees. If he refused the case, Jack could be alerting the cartels of past and present dealings with clients as flippers. It would not sit well with Moses's bosses and would endanger the lives of both Moses and Keegan, and perhaps others who had referred bosses to Keegan. Jack had to move forward and figure it out as he went.

Chapter 14

Working the Case

The Elrod Moses case was assigned to the courtroom of Judge Angus Baldwin—the same courtroom where Raphael Martinez's case landed. It would be a different result this time, Keegan thought.

Keegan met with Gatlin Driscoll, the AUSA assigned to prosecute Elrod Moses. Driscoll was yet another young prosecutor determined to prove himself to his peers. He was vigorous in all his assignments, a no-deal kind of guy.

"Mr. Driscoll," said Jack, starting his introduction, "Jack Keegan, attorney for Elrod Moses. How are you today?"

"Very good, Mr. Keegan. I was just looking over the Moses file and find that we have a solid case here. What can I do for you?"

"You know Moses's background but let me fill you in about mine and my relationship with Moses," Jack began. "My contempt for drug dealers is well established. You are not about to bring me to see things as you see them. You would be preaching to the choir," said Jack to loosen Driscoll up.

"I spent a great deal of time cultivating a team who assisted me and the DEA to bring down major players here and in Mexico—a mission that severely disrupted cartel operations along the Gulf Coast and drug trafficking to the United States. Elrod Moses was an important team member. He put his life on the line for us and was successful in his assignments. You can check out the operation that was codenamed 'Operation Wetsuit.'

"I am asking that you check into that and extend a little consideration for his significant cooperation with us," Jack pleaded.

"No need, Mr. Keegan. That was then, and this is now. No deals will be made on past performance. We may use him again. That is what we will check into, a whole new cooperation agreement. Okay?" Gatlin Driscoll said smugly.

"Please keep an open mind and let me know what you can do. I can be reached anytime."

Jack knew Moses's cooperation in a new mission would not play out well for anyone, including Jack. If his boss discovered Moses's deception, he and Keegan would both end up in the Miami waterways. Jack poured over his discovery material and started his own investigation. He knew that hand-to-hand deliveries were difficult to beat, but could there have been entrapment or some other defense that could be successfully argued? Entrapment is never an easy defense to argue. Enforcement protocol generally would be the better play. Who were the witnesses who set Moses up for his fall? Jack started digging. First things first: who are the arresting agents?

Ford Wilson was the lead agent on paper. He was a fourteen-year veteran of the DEA and living large for his pay grade. He traveled regularly but unpredictably to Mexico and the Cayman Islands. His wife and two teen kids always stayed back home in Miami.

Angel Gonzales was Wilson's most frequent partner. He was also involved in Elrod Moses's sting operation arrest. Angel was a DEA agent for only a few years and had extended family and property in Michoacán, Mexico. His immediate family, his wife and three young kids, lived in Miami near Wilson.

The buyers who were staged to purchase product from Moses were all introduced by snitches—cooperating informants groomed by Wilson and Gonzales. Jack learned that there were lapses in discoverable recordings made during drug transactions with Moses. Also, Keegan noticed the arrest reports identified only the two agents, but Moses said there were three different buyers and snitches at each staged deal. There had to be another agent unnamed in the reports.

It was time to contact his former mission compadre, DEA Agent Ariana De Leon. Jack started with the niceties expected in reigniting a conversation with an old friend and lover, when Ariana so typically stopped him to get to the point:

"What's up, Jack? What can I do for you?"

Jack told her about his case and the two identified agents involved in Moses's arrest. She, of course, knew Moses and the contributions he'd made to her old mission team. She also knew of the agents. They were suspected for a while of being on the take to facilitate drug operations in Mexico. It was an ongoing investigation that she could not discuss, but her confirmation of Jack's suspicions sent him further into his investigation.

Keegan searched property ownership records and, what little he could get, financial records of the two arresting agents. He discovered a plethora of information that would support additional discovery motions that he prepared but did not file with the court. Jack made another appointment to see AUSA Gatlin Driscoll.

"We need to revisit the Moses case, Mr. Driscoll. I have information about your arresting agents that should prove helpful in our defense. Additional discovery motions have been prepared to compel release of financial information that appears to involve cartel payoffs. I thought that we could discuss things again before filing our motions.

"It seems that Agent Ford Wilson, while living modestly in Miami, has substantial accounts building up in the Cayman Islands. Agent Angel Gonzales's extended family is living uncharacteristically quite large in Michoacán on property cash-purchased and owned by Gonzales. You have a couple of bad agents here on cartel payrolls. It needs to be exposed."

"Don't file your motions. I'll look into it and get back to you," Driscoll assured Keegan.

Jack discussed his discovery progress with Moses that gave Moses some encouragement, but not enough to be confident. It was not only the agents that were seemingly tied to a cartel but also their snitches. He knew right away that there was cartel competition that was afoot. Moses reported the information back to his boss.

It was only a few days later, early morning, while Jack was pouring over papers in his office when he got a call from AUSA Driscoll.

"Mr. Keegan, Gatlin Driscoll. I need to meet with you   regarding our last conversation. Do you have time today?"

"3 o'clock?" offered Jack. "Fine, see you here at three."

Keegan was apprehensive and didn't know what to expect. He probably should have said he'd be right over, rather than to allow his apprehension to build all day. It was 2:45 p.m. when Jack arrived. 2:59 p.m. Driscoll walked out of his office and greeted him again in the lobby.

"Come on in, Mr. Keegan."

"Please call me Jack."

They sat momentarily at Driscoll's desk. Driscoll was silent and somber as he stared at the top of his desk. A minute or so passed.

"It has come to my attention that two of our agents are missing and have not left word with anyone—the same two agents we spoke of right here in my office a few days ago. We are also trying to locate three key witnesses in the Moses case. I am inclined to believe you may be responsible, Mr. Keegan."

"My God, Gatlin, I hate that you even think that. What is happening here? I haven't said a thing that would encourage this to happen,"

Jack said with a quiver.

Jack Keegan was stunned and left Gatlin Driscoll's office. He was puzzled by the news. Keegan's mind was spinning to recall the specifics of his last conversation with Elrod Moses. He wanted to know if the agents were killed. Were the witnesses? He knew he shouldn't ask. But he also knew that nobody escapes the wrath of law-enforcement vengeance if a cop or agent gets killed.

But it was different in this case. Those agents were seemingly in bed with a cartel, on their payroll. If true, they were even dirtier than the cartel. It was a position they chose to be in. And the snitches? Well, who really cares about them? It could be argued that justice was served by their presumed demise. The DEA gets to clean house, a few more dealers are off the streets, Keegan wins his case and gets to keep his handsome fees— not to mention his life! Moses moves on to make more money for his bosses. Everyone gets their just rewards, Keegan thought.

Also, what about the suspected unknown third buyer that Moses spoke of? Who was he? Was he an agent? A CI? Why would only he not be listed on paper? Were agents and witnesses killed or just missing during competitive cartel warfare? Keegan had to investigate further. He knew, however, that he should not dig too deeply into cartel business.

Chapter 15

Working with Clients

Elrod Moses was called back to Jack's office. Jack directed Moses to answer only the questions he would ask of him.

"Sit down, my friend. We need to talk," Jack directed Moses.

"I am not asking you to tell me anything about business operations, but I need you to give me details about only activities that occurred before and during your arrest and only persons present at those times and all conversations relating to the deals. What happened following your arrest is not my concern, nor should it be yours right now. Okay?"

Elrod Moses began:

"One of our street workers, Emiliano Pena, brought a buyer to me in a deal that went down mid-June in Little Havana.

"I knew him as Paco, but the arrest report identifies him as arresting DEA Agent Ford Wilson. We closed the deal for 5,000 grams of MDMA. Our end took in $75K for $150,000 street value. "The second deal went down two weeks later with Jesse, identified in the report as DEA Agent Angel Gonzales. He paid me $80,000 for 700 grams of crack. The street value was $175,000. I thought he was okay too. Jesse was brought to me by a trusted Miami worker, Emilio Ramos. We did the deal again in Little Havana. "There was a third deal that was planned much earlier but did not go down until two days later. It was the big one. It went down near the lighthouse at the northern tip of Bill Baggs State Park in Key Biscayne. The buyer identified himself only as Cruz. As you may know, he is a ghost on paper. He brought 3.5 mil to the table for 5,000 grams of cocaine and 800 grams of fentanyl. Cruz was intro- duced to me by Sebastian Fuentes, who came to the drop with Emilio Ramos. Cruz held all the money himself for the transfer. When the product was transferred for the cases of cash, Gonzales and Wilson moved in for the bust. Cruz disappeared without the cash or drugs. I was placed under arrest along with Ramos and

Fuentes. To my knowledge, neither the drugs nor cash was inventoried. I am sure you noticed the same."

"Hold on, Elrod. You're sure Cruz didn't leave with the cash he brought?"

"Yes, sir!"

"And you, Fuentes, and Ramos were scooped away before the cash was seized?"

"Yes, sir! Two cases of cash, 3.5 million, still on the ground."

"The product?"

"Still on the ground."

"And Wilson and Gonzales were exclusively in control of the three of you and the whole area around you?"

"Yes, sir!"

"Did they collect the $75K and $80K payments you received on the first two buys?"

"No, sir. Those were gone—sent to the Man."

"So, the feds have no cash inventoried, just the drugs on the first two buys, and no witnesses?"

"Looks like it."

"Okay, Elrod. We'll talk later. Soon. I'll give you a call."

Jack's instincts were piqued. It just wasn't right. Nothing happens this way by chance. Suspicions grew. Why is Elrod Moses the last man standing?

All ethical considerations about serving your client and confidentiality be damned, Keegan had to know what he unwittingly became involved in when undertaking this case. He would follow the money—and the bodies, if any. Jack had to protect himself.

How could Elrod Moses lose at least 3.5 million dollars' worth of drugs and still be worthy of Keegan's representation in a case where there is no property to recover or a viable winning of indentured servitude? Cartels are profit-only oriented and will cut their losses in a heartbeat. Moses had to know this. Why is he still in the game?

Because he *IS* the game, Jack thought. His client must be moving up to compete in the big game. He is taking on a cartel. Moses was playing his bosses. *Not a good idea for him, nor for me*, Keegan thought.

Jack Keegan was cunning. He had more street knowledge than intellect, but it suited him best in his line of work. He was always able to see things as they were without the intellectual discourse muddying up the conversation. He got to the point without losing his focus. He was ahead of his peers and competitors. Moses was his latest challenge to not only survive but also to land on top, taking on the criminal minions who would have it otherwise.

Chapter 16

Investigating the Case

Jack Keegan had to call in favors from prior occupational contacts to gather more information about the agents and the associates of Elrod Moses. He no longer had access to needed information but knew who did. Keegan dug deeper into the activities of his client and of his client's associates—and of agents Ford Wilson and Angel Gonzales. And who is Cruz?

Keegan had to reach back to Agent Ariana De Leon who had been, since his last conversation with her, promoted to Special Agent in Charge of the Miami Field Division, and who had already denied Jack information in an ongoing investigation of the agents. She was the best he knew to get the answers he needed. He called to meet up with her again.

"Ariana, I realize your position here, but I need your help. I think you may also use my help. I think we have some rogue players that may be branching off from the cartels."

The meeting was all business without the awkward flirtations of the past. Jack was still smitten with Ariana, but he knew that he had to offer Ariana more than a compliment to enlist her cooperation. He promised to offer up evidence of his client, Elrod Moses, if he was involved in staging his own case. He also promised unrestricted access to his case files on Moses, a breach of confidentiality that Keegan knew might come back to hurt him.

"Okay, Jack. I'll do this for you. I'll do this for the agency. I trust your cooperation and will do what I can," Ariana assured Jack. "I'll get ahold of AUSA Gatlin Driscoll and tell him we are on the case together. He will advise against your involvement, but I'll vouch for your credibility."

"Thank you, Ariana. You're the best!"

Keegan had to review his strategies that could, if unsuccessful, end his law practice if not his life. He knew that the strategies' "ends" would justify the "means" to absolve him of breaching his client's confidentiality only if Moses was in the process of committing more crimes, of staging his arrest to assume another criminal enterprise. It was a stretch to assume, but Keegan's instincts were keen. Keegan also knew that if he didn't stop Moses from carrying it off, Moses's drug-supplying cartel would hold Keegan responsible.

Jack Keegan kept notes from his days working missions with the DEA. He used his informants, Martinez, Lopez, and Moses, against Echevarria and knew that when Mendez took over the Echevarria cartel operations, the Mendez cartel made Martinez, Lopez, and Moses new drug-distributing soldiers for the Mendez cartel. Jack heard that they'd received some perks from the takeover but not enough to assure their loyalty. Would Echevarria's takedown embolden Keegan's snitches to build their own empire? Would his takedown embolden DEA agents to get in the game on the other side? It was less than a week later that Ariana would again meet with Jack. It was less of a meeting place than Jack had expected.

"Meet me at the corner of Wade and Vine at 7 p.m."

Really, Jack thought. What is this, a suspense novel? It must be, but he couldn't deny the excitement of reliving his past.

Keegan followed directions to meet at a dilapidated building that he thought was condemned, or should have been, in the fashion of a Hollywood drama that would portray a doomed presence.

"Who is paying you to represent Elrod Moses, Jack? I expect you're getting big money. Is it the Mendez cartel?" Ariana asked. "Is Moses reaching in his own pockets for any of this?"

"Elrod walked in with some of it. I set my fee. He brought the rest. Sometimes I get a call from a concerned party that I believe is his cartel boss. Nobody talks about money, just about expected case results and evidence against my client," Jack explained. "They don't seem to care about cost as long as they will see a greater return on their investment with their man back on the street when the case ends."

"I would like to hook Moses up to a lie box," Ariana requested. "Would he agree? Would you?"

"That would not be a good idea, Ariana. I would rather find his workers for information. Any idea where Wilson and Gonzales may be?

How about the bagman, Cruz? Do we know who he is?" Jack asked.

"Wilson and Gonzales are both gone. Their Miami homes are vacant. Their bank and all service accounts are closed. Wilson's wife and children are also missing. The Wilsons have two teen children and no known extended family. Gonzales is nowhere to be found, but his wife and three young kids are living in Michoacán on property cash-purchased and owned by Gonzales. His extended family is also living in Mexico. It appears that Wilson cashed out of a stockpile of liquid investments in the Cayman Islands. Both look very suspicious. I have no information on Cruz.

"That's all I can report right now," said Ariana.

"Okay, keep me posted," said Jack. "Thanks."

As soon as he left Ariana, Keegan called his favorite client, Raphael Martinez, for additional information. Did he know Cruz? Sure! Raphael responded immediately and came right into Jack's office.

"Cruz? You mean Santiago De la Cruz?"

"Maybe I do, El. Who is he?" Jack asked.

"Cruz works for the Reyes cartel. They were squeezed out of their east coast operations during the Mendez takeover of the Echevarria cartel.

"Reyes is now operating exclusively along Mexico's west coast from Nayarit to Tapachula. They are headquartered near Michoacán. Word has it they are competing with the Mendez cartel for distribution routes and destinations. They are also recruiting for soldiers."

"Do you know what Elrod Moses is doing?" Jack Keegan asked El, but knowing the answer before being told.

"Sure, he signed up a while ago after our mission together. How's he doing?" Raphael asked in passing.

"Not bad," Jack remarked. "He's adjusting."

"Let's have that drink we are always agreeing to but never seem to enjoy together. We have certainly been through the best and worst of times together, haven't we?" Raphael remarked.

"I may need your help on this one. Can I count on you, El? I need a friend who can protect me this time, a friend who can see danger coming and protect me against the consequences of an unfair result. Please help me," Jack pleaded.

"That's a switch, Jack. I help you? Sounds desperate, but sure, I'll have your back."

Jack Keegan was upset at the news but intrigued as to how this would all play out. He had a client charged with serious deliveries, no evidence of value against him, a handsome retainer to win the case against his client, and a cartel breathing down his neck.

Anyone want to go deep-sea fishing? Jack thought, amusing himself with his own morbid humor.

Suspicions that the disappearing players were murdered in Elrod Moses's arrest were evaporating. Keegan began to realize that there was a personnel change between the cartels that Jack himself had facilitated in his old mission with the DEA. The rogue agents and Elrod Moses, possibly with his accomplices Fuentes and Ramos, sought greener pastures with the Reyes cartel and set everything up, striking a blow to the Mendez cartel in the process. Or perhaps Fuentes and Ramos were not in on the plan.

If Keegan's suspicions were true, the rogue agents Wilson and Gonzalez planned to leave the DEA for a more lucrative lifestyle. They were in danger of retribution from the Mendez cartel but would be found in the location and under the protection of the Reyes cartel. Elrod Moses, Fuentes, and Ramos, on the other hand, if Jack's suspicions were true, would be left mostly unprotected in Miami, importing product from the Reyes cartel for distribution in competition with loyal Mendez soldiers. Moses and the others were relying on the Mendez bosses believing the staged arrest was real and the money and drugs were confiscated by the feds.

But Fuentes and Ramos are missing following their arrest. Did they flee to the Reyes cartel territory as did the agents, presumably? Or are they to be found dead in the Florida waterways? If the latter, their deaths would have been at the hand of Moses. Keegan suspects that he needs to figure things out before the Mendez cartel. He needs to get answers from Moses. He would enlist Raphael Martinez to help him.

Keegan asked Martinez to meet at a concession stand along Virginia Key Beach Park at the entry of the Rickenbacker Causeway that would take you to Key Biscayne. He would be meeting Elrod Moses there for a private talk. Moses would be unaware that Martinez would be joining the meeting for Jack's protection if needed. The meeting could not have been at Jack's office; he wanted to assure that there would be no audio or video surveillance.

It was a beautiful view of Miami from the shores of Virginia Beach. It was very private, especially on Sunday at 7:00 p.m. when the meeting was scheduled. Moses showed up on time and alone. Martinez was with Jack when Moses arrived.

"What's this, Jack? How's it going, El? Are we going to start a campfire for a bonding moment to sing 'Kumbaya'?" Elrod Moses quipped. "I thought we were meeting privately."

"What's wrong, El," Raphael asked, using his own nickname on Elrod, "aren't you glad to see me? It's been a long time. It's good to see you."

"I asked Raphael to come to help sort things out in your case. Your case is not one I can send my investigator on. We aren't sure what will surface, and we can't ask for better help than from someone in your line of work. I have questions and think you have answers. There are things I have to know now for the well-being of both of us," Jack said urgently. "We both have to get out of this alive."

Keegan continued, "We know the DEA agents Wilson and Gonzales are dirty. If they are alive, they are with Santiago De la Cruz, a soldier in the Reyes cartel, the bogus agent who left you in the custody of Wilson and Gonzales following your third transaction. If Fuentes and Ramos are alive, they are also with or near them in Mexico. If so, they will someday be picked up on bond forfeiture arrest warrants. All suspicion is on you for being the last man standing without drugs, money, or answers. That will not play well for both of us. Your case may be dismissed, but all eyes will be on you until answers are obtained. Don't think you will be able to conduct business again. Don't think your bosses won't suspect what the feds are thinking. Don't think you won't be questioned extensively by Mendez. Don't think I won't be. Let's face it, you're fucked. I'm fucked. I am the only one who can try to clear this up. I am the only one. Let's go now! Tell me."

"I thought I could do this, Jack," Elrod said with his head almost in his lap. "The cops told me the plan. It was as you said. But I thought I could make it better for me. It was my chance to branch out on my own. I would have it all."

That was all Martinez was allowed to hear. Jack moved close to Elrod, away from Martinez.

"You motherfucking piece of shit; let me have him, Jack. I'll take care of this asshole," Raphael Martinez said while lunging at Elrod's throat.

"Easy, El. We need him, and he needs me," Jack said to calm Raphael and comfort Elrod. "We have to fix this right!"

Jack Keegan leaned in closer to Elrod to ask in a whisper, "Are the agents dead?"

"Yes, sir."

"Are Fuentes, and Ramos?"

"Yes, sir."

"Is Santiago De la Cruz?"

"No, sir. He left before everything went down," Elrod assured. "Wilson and Gonzales were to take the money and drugs and meet back up with Cruz. They were planning to split the money in Mexico. The drugs would be resold by the Reyes cartel, who would also take back the money they fronted. I wouldn't get much out of the deal."

"Where did everyone go after your arrest?" asked Jack.

"Not sure, Jack. Home?" Elrod said with the little humor he could still muster.

"You motherfucker. I'll mess you up!" exclaimed Raphael, ready to pounce.

"Thank you, Rafi"—being the first time Jack called Rafael that nickname to avoid confusion with Elrod's. "I will take this from here. Thank you for coming tonight. All will be well here."

Rafael Martinez stormed away without acknowledgement of either Jack or Elrod. He was slighted that he was not called upon to exercise the powers of persuasion that Jack seemingly called upon in his invitation to the meeting. Jack had other plans, though. Jack comforted Elrod into a false sense of security.

"What do you say we stroll along the beach? We have a lot to discuss about our plans, don't we?"

"Sure do, boss. What are we going to do?"

"I think we just let them wonder what all went down. What do you think?" Jack said comfortingly.

"Where are the drugs and money now?" Keegan asked.

"I have them stashed with Manuel Lopez, who I brought in on the plan. You know him, right? He worked with us on our DEA mission. We hooked up on this. He helped me intercept the cash and product and dispose of the evidence, you know—all loose ends," Moses said with pride, not realizing how stupid he was.

"And where are Lopez, the product, and the cash?" Jack needed to know.

"In a vacant house in Stiltsville, waiting for my case to resolve so we can get the hell out of here," Moses exclaimed.

"I need to talk with Manuel Lopez. We will both go there tonight. Where will we go exactly?" Keegan asked.

"I'll have to show you, Jack. It's hard to reach, and you need a boat."

Stiltsville was a perfect place to hide out, Jack thought. The wood vacant houses, a dwindling community of homes built in the ocean on stilts in the early 1930s, are located about one mile south of Cape Florida on the edge of Biscayne Bay. Most of the houses were destroyed by a hurricane in 1965.

"Okay, Moses, but I will have to call you when I get a boat and have a little more time. It won't be tonight. We can get through this," Jack said, knowing all too well that Elrod could not be saved, nor could Manuel Lopez.

Jack Keegan had to clean the slate with Moses. They would undoubtedly be questioned by both the Mendez and Reyes cartels. Moses's plan to go rogue, and all things that Keegan participated in with Moses against the Echevarria, Reyes, and Mendez cartels during his mission with the DEA, would surely be revealed. Moses would fold like a deck of cards. Plenty of people would be questioned and go down with him, including Keegan. Something had to be done with Elrod and, of course, Manuel Lopez.

A call to Martinez would explain the desperation Jack felt. Raphael knew instinctively what had to be done. He felt Jack's desperation to be marching orders against Elrod, although nothing was ever expressed. But first, Keegan had to get rid of Moses's case.

Jack would not reveal Moses's confession and pending demise to anyone. Upon returning to his office, Jack left a message for Ariana to meet with him there. She would come to his office the next day. He was cordial and, being his old self, excessively complimentary to her. She sensed that he was calmer and more confident this time, however. Ariana, of course, got right to the point.

"So, what do you have for me, Jack? Are you sharing?"

"The third buyer, 'Cruz,' was in fact a Reyes cartel soldier named Santiago De la Cruz. I hear he is from Guatemala and was brought up north to Jalisco to oversee Reyes' operations. Your agents, and maybe Cruz, evidently set up the buys to abscond with the cash and drugs seized."

"'Evidently'? What does that mean?" Ariana asked.

"I haven't been able to reach anyone to confirm anything, but it all adds up with Santiago De la Cruz in the mix," Jack replied. "In my opinion, Reyes is retaliating against Mendez for squeezing them out of the Gulf. In any event, I need to get this Moses case dropped, being that there is no evidence against him. Just doing my job, Ariana."

Rather than filing his previously prepared motions, Keegan just motioned the case up before Judge Angus Baldwin for a dismissal. AUSA Driscoll was served proper notice, and Keegan had Elrod Moses by his side. Driscoll conceded merely an evidentiary problem in the case and asked that the case be dismissed without prejudice so that it might be brought back if proper evidence surfaced. The case was so dismissed without prejudice.

Moses was free to go with his posted bond to be refunded. Jack Keegan had won another case before Judge Baldwin under the same suspicious circumstances as was the case against Martinez. It was a pattern that was all too frequent in the courts of the Southern District of Florida. Suspicious cases were common in the Southern District, however, Jack thought. This federal district has the dubious distinction of having had more judges removed from the bench through impeachment than any other district.

———～～～———

Jack Keegan never set up that meeting with Moses so he could talk with Lopez. He thought he didn't have to because, following Moses's case dismissal, Raphael Martinez was expected to meet up with Moses and Lopez. Jack didn't want any discussion with Martinez about the issue, but it appeared to Jack that the coast would be clear.

Neither Moses nor Lopez was heard from again, and the money and drugs were never recovered. The cartels seemingly never knew what happened to anyone or anything. The mystery was never solved, but Jack Keegan won his case again, and his unblemished law practice was still doing well.

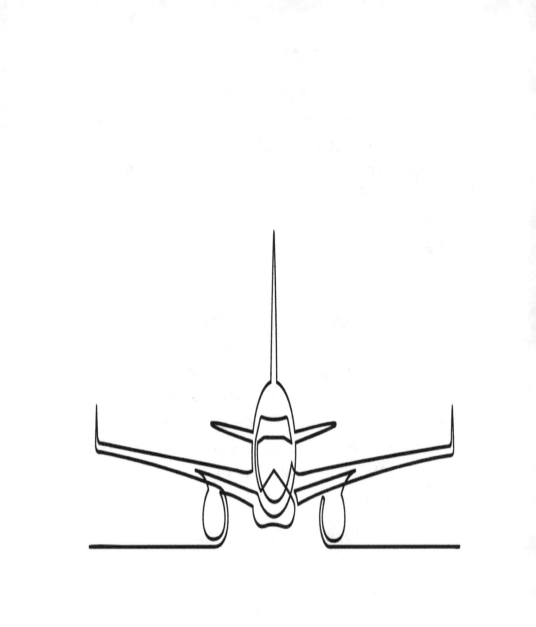

Chapter 17

Leaving Miami

Jack Keegan was tired of the dangers of getting so close to cartels' business. He liked the fees but missed the comparative simplicity of representing clients in Chicago. Street gangs were not as sophisticated and were more predictable in Chicago. Criminal defense attorneys in Chicago did not as often have to look over their shoulders as they did in Miami. The drug possessions and distributions were much smaller and did not usually arouse the attention of cartels.

It was more comfortable in Chicago. Cases were won and lost on the merits. The evidence and arguments prevailed more than "under-the-table, unethical tactics" that were so pervasive in Miami.

Keegan wondered why the feds didn't move into Miami after homing in on Chicago to fight judicial corruption. He thought perhaps that the cartels' reach would be too dangerous of an adversary to tackle. Stepping on toes in Miami would probably bring too much bad publicity and reveal too much corruption that would unsettle the powers that be.

Jack decided to keep an office presence in Miami, however, for the irresistible cases that might come his way. He contacted his friend and Miami mentor, Art Zimmerman.

"Good morning, Art," Jack started the conversation. "I hope   all is well with you and wanted to tell you that I will be mostly in Chicago again. I hope also that we can get together on cases that I can bring to you if they arise. I may also appear alone on some of the easier ones that would require only a short stay here in Miami."

"Of course, Jack. You are always welcome to share my office if you need. I will be at your beck and call if you let me know you're coming down here. You made quite a splash on the cases you handled here. No pun intended. You do damn good work."

"Thanks, Art. You gave me sound advice and direction. I appreciate it."

"No problem, Jack. Have a safe trip back home. I hope to see you again soon."

It seemed to Jack that all would be simple in Chicago compared to the shenanigans that he witnessed in Miami and now that the feds had finished up their Operation Greylord investigation in Chicago. It would be good to be home.

It was before Keegan left for home, however, that he received a call asking for his representation in a major drug deal with multiple murders in the notorious gang-ravaged Chicago Englewood neighborhood. He discovered that all defendants were then on bond and said he would return the call when he settled in back home. It was difficult for Jack to return to the grind of office work so soon. He had a colleague meet with the prospective clients to gather preliminary information about the case. He needed some downtime first with his family.

Oh, yes—his family! Jack's work had always consumed Jack's time and efforts. His work took him away from his family way too often. But just as he was raised with his sister by a loving family, his family was the core of all that he loved, of all that he cherished. He settled down after law school to marry the girl who stole his heart. Two sons and a daughter later, all going to college to pursue their dreams in different directions, Jack became more involved in their career decisions.

Jack's wife, Elizabeth, was his sole inspiration. She always took care of things at home and gave Jack her encouragement to move forward in his endeavors. She was his rock, as beautiful as she was strong in her support.

Amanda was his youngest daughter, a sweetheart that stole Jack's heart. She was the favored one. His love for her was fueled by her commonsense approach to everything, even as a child. She never whined to get her way. She was always patient and appreciated all that came to her, which was mostly anything she wanted.

Jack's sons were as different as one could imagine. Jack, Jr., was a carbon copy of Jack. He had the pragmatic justification for everything. Nothing could be as clear to him as a situation that called for justice— a justice that brought a clear resolution to what was right and wrong, a justice that was practical.

Ambrose, however, was a true believer in just pursuits. He fought hard for the under-privileged. He fought for the forgotten ones. He was a "do-gooder" who would be scorned by the pragmatist cops, who would shun his ideals.

Amanda did more than Ambrose in bringing everyone to the table. She was the motivator of true justice. She showed Jack, her father, that more could be gained from the scraps of compassionate compromise than could be found in the heap of success. In other words, help the downtrodden to lift themselves up. Their social contribution will be soon realized. She was more like Ambrose than Jack, Jr., or her father.

It was Jack Keegan and his inspiring family that brought light to the otherwise dark issues. Jack often preached,

"We must always use our common sense to find the truth. It has been said that our ex-istence depends on it. We cannot give just lip service to that; we must live the truth to prove that it is real. We are the testimony of fact—testimony that will cause others to see things as they really are."

He knew that he was being preachy and philosophical, but Jack wanted to stress to his children the importance of ferreting out lies and inaccuracies that could keep them from finding the truth that would properly guide them and others.

———

Jack's family gathered for his return home as if he had been away for years. He was welcomed as a prodigal husband and father who seemingly abandoned them for too long. Maybe he did. He always thought he did what was best for his family.

His family embraced him as if he were a stranger. He felt that he was, being that they were so grown up and that he missed so much of their journey.

"How is school? What is everyone doing lately? It's good to be back home," Jack asked and said in an awkward way to greet family.

Jack, Jr., was proud to jump into the conversation to tell of his latest law school studies and commented on his academic achievements. Ambrose added his two cents, bragging about his involvement in the latest social movement. Amanda just stood quietly aside, smiling her satisfaction that all were there together.

Elizabeth greeted Jack more genuinely and lovingly. They'd really missed each other. There was nothing better than to be back home with her.

Chapter 18

Being with Family

After his R & R at home with his family, Jack went to his downtown office to dust things off and get things moving again. He didn't realize when he left Chicago that Miami cases would take up so much of his time. Jack, Jr., asked to join him to get a feel for the practice of law that he was about to undertake with his soon-to-be-earned sheepskin under his belt. Jack was not crazy about Junior entering his criminal defense practice, though. He did not think he had the fortitude and maturity to handle it. But he agreed to show Junior the ropes. He was twenty-five and near ready to apply his new professional learning.

Looking around his Chicago office, Jack realized that he needed more room, especially if he were to take on an associate. He was impressed with the criminal defense law firms of Miami, like Zimmerman's, that were set up to office five or more attorneys. Jack opened up the back storage area to make room for another office. Jack moved his mediocre desk into the second office and purchased a desk and chair that he is still enjoying today. They were a seven-foot dark mahogany desk with brass and leather inlay and an oversized tufted brown leather chair. His newly remodeled offices would now have generous room for Junior if he should decide to join him permanently.

Elizabeth and Amanda joined them to help get things started again. They sorted files and arranged books to make it easier for them. Amanda envied her brother's new journey with her father and thought about becoming a lawyer herself. She said so while straightening her father's office. Amanda was twenty, still in undergraduate school contemplating her future.

"Why not, Amanda?" her father said. "You would be a great lawyer. It is apparent that you would have trial skills, but you know you don't have to be a litigator. There are many areas of practice that you could pursue."

"I just might. We'll see," said Amanda.

Ambrose had received his bachelor's degree in Social Studies, consistent with his aspirations for social change. He had no desire to study law. He believed more in anarchy than the structure of rules and law. Jack accepted that he was doing what he thought was right and knew that he would still obey the rules and laws that he so often opposed.

Jack, Jr., was excited to join his father and looked forward to being mentored in the practice of law. It would be the real-world application of all the rules and concepts that had caused a lot of academic confusion. He could never remember constitutional precepts and conditions that were seemingly so contradictory in court rulings. He asked his father,

"When do we know when something violates someone's constitutional rights? Sometimes both sides assert their rights over the same event or incident. Isn't it sometimes hard to find an argument that makes clear what a case outcome should be?"

"It is, Son. And even courts sometimes lose sight of the just application of the law and our Constitution. There is always an argument when you can convince the court that what you are advocating would bring a ruling in your client's case that would be a fair and just result. When you cannot argue a specific statute or constitutional issue with precise clarity, argue *'fairness.'* Many cases have been won by convincing the trier of fact and law that an outcome other than what you're urging would be unfair.

"It stuck with me what my constitutional law professor said in law school:

Remember this: One's constitutional rights end at the tip of another's nose.

"He said it in a way that was most clear and directory in my criminal defense practice. You won't always find clear answers, but neither will the courts. We are all imperfect beings and need to step back to reflect on the real consequences of case outcomes. Decisions need to balance, and sometimes prioritize, rights to bring order and justice.

"There are no black-and-white answers for everything. And advocates need to understand the merits of compromise prior to trial to avoid uncertain and sometimes misguided rulings that would otherwise disrupt the social balance of rights."

"You make it sound easy, Dad," Jack, Jr., said, being satisfied with the clarity.

"It is anything but easy, Junior," his father answered.

Amanda listened closely to her dad's answer to her brother's question and for the first time realized the philosophical art of being a lawyer. She trashed her notion of a lawyer's mercenary and unethical behavior being the standard operating procedure in the practice of law. Surely there would be many to fit the unkind stereotype, but she discovered a noble purpose in practicing law that she'd never realized before. That simple dialogue between her father and brother would motivate her to pursue her future in the study of law.

Amanda finished up her helpful sorting of things in her father's newly remodeled offices and left with her mother and brother to go home. Jack remained to review work files that needed to be done. He leaned back at his new desk and felt home again. He would take occasional cases in Miami, but not like the ones he had. He counted on Art Zimmerman to handle those cases.

Before calling his new client that was screened and waiting for his return to Chicago, Jack thought he'd check in with his sister, Carol, whom he hadn't seen nor heard from in a while. Carol was enjoying her life raising two boys and a girl, all of whom were sure to have a successful future. Carol married a respected judge, and her sons were starting law school. With no prior family members ever holding professional college degrees, Jack and his sister were the first to do so, and in getting their kids ready to start their own large family law firm. Except that Carol became a college mathematics professor, of all things, and her daughter, Kate, became a teacher after first pursuing an acting career in Hollywood. They were all happy to be living a good and enviable life—as was Jack and his family.

"Hello, Carol. Jack here. How are you and your wonderful family? I'm back from Miami and looking forward to concentrating my law practice here in Chicago."

"Good to hear from you, Jack. We are all doing fine and miss seeing you and yours," said

Carol. "Let's all get together and catch up. Next Sunday at 5? I'm cooking."

"Sounds good; see you Sunday afternoon at 5:00 p.m."

Jack and Carol continued small talk and family updates but cut the conversation short to save it for their dinner gathering the following Sunday. It was even better to be back home after talking with her and to gather with her family. There is no place like home.

A call was then placed to DeShawn Robinson, a Disciples lieutenant gangbanger. He was surprisingly on bond for multiple murders in a drive-by shooting along the Eisenhower Expressway. The victims and alleged offenders were all from the gang-ravaged Englewood neighborhood on Chicago's south side. No other defendant was captured. Three known suspects got away. An appointment was set to meet in Jack's office. A handsome retainer was to be paid at that time in certified funds. That's the way it works.

Jack did not have his son present at the initial meeting. He wanted to be sure that he had control of the prospective client and could handle the client's temperament. It was that way meeting new clients with violent cases, although it was not as stressful as dealing with cartels.

They met, and the rules requiring the reporting of large cash payments were understood. It had to be understood that the case would be concluded at adjudication and would require additional fees if any post-trial motions or appeals were filed. Robinson knew the drill. He was a six-time loser for violent crimes, including murder. Jack again wondered why Robinson was released on bond. It would have been much different when Jack was a cop. New times, new rules.

Jack, Jr., joined his father at the next office meeting with the client. Other than that, all meetings would be at court, on scheduled court dates, until trial preparation, if any was necessary, that would be again at Jack's office. There would be no house calls in Englewood. Jack's client intake protocol was standard. It was necessary to follow not only for safety but also to make sure he was paid before undertaking a case.

Another call came into the office while Jack and Junior were discussing business. The call from Juan Pablo and Delfina Jiménez was placed on speakerphone. They explained in broken English the husband's situation that led to his arrest. Delfina did most of the talking being that Juan Pablo's English was so poor. It was unclear if he was a victim or offender in a street robbery. He said that he merely resisted the attack, defending himself by drawing his own gun that he admittedly carried illegally. Juan Pablo said the robber was shot and killed by him in an exchange of gunfire between them. It was unclear as to who provoked the attack and for what purpose. Both men had a criminal history of violence. Both men had their guns drawn against each other during the robbery. Both men could be seen as aggressive offenders.

During the gunfire exchange, a young girl bystander was also killed by a stray bullet. Jiménez was the only one left to be charged. Public outcry prevented otherwise.

It would be a learning case not only for Junior, but also Jack felt this would be interesting for Amanda to sit in on. Amanda, a non-lawyer, was hired for this case to investigate for Jack. There would be no confidentiality ethical concerns being that she was a firm employee and equally bound to the confidentiality of their work product. The facts and circumstances were unclear but so far uncontested due to Juan Pablo's criminal history and his inability to speak English. A deadly crime was committed, and Jiménez was the one left standing to pay the consequences.

Expected legal fees were advised and the conversation went silent. Delfina said in a soft, almost inaudible voice,

"We're sorry, Mr. Keegan, we can't afford that. Thank you for taking your time to talk with us."

"Wait just a minute," said Jack. "I have a few more questions. Have you yet spoken to other attorneys about this?"

"A few," said Delfina.

"What did they quote you, and what did they tell you to expect in the defense of Juan Pablo's case?"

"They all said it would cost less, but they said my husband   would have to go to jail for some time. They would work things out in court," she sighed.

"And what do you both do for a living? Do you own a home? How much do you make? What savings do you have? Do you have kids? Do you support anyone else?" Jack asked in a series of follow-up questions that would influence his willingness to help them.

They were poor. They both worked minimum-wage jobs and supported extended family living with them in a rented apartment. Jack decided to take the case "pro bono," free of legal fees, not only in consideration of the clients, but also for the learning experience to enlighten Jack, Jr., Amanda, and perhaps even Ambrose to the social good and justice that could be achieved in the practice of law.

Amanda was assigned the task of gathering all information she could about Juan Pablo's life and the experiences that brought him to the case at hand. She was to discuss what she gathered with Jack, Jr., before bringing it to her father for his review. She was excited to be an integral part of the defense in the case. Jack was proud to bring her aboard.

The case of People v. Juan Pablo Jiménez was first prepared in courtroom 101 of the Criminal Courts Building for assignment to a felony trial court. The first formal appearance in the case was for arraignment before The Honorable Judge Lincoln Davis. Jack and Junior had to prepare the preliminary motions that would register their court appearance and their request for discovery materials. They would wait for Amanda's report and defense materials before discussing the Jiménez case further. In the meantime, they moved on to other case files.

The DeShawn Robinson case was pulled for review. Jack and Junior sat together to discuss the prosecution's evidence. Jack started,

"It appears that no eyewitnesses of any significance came forward here. The prosecution got only inexact descriptions of involved vehicles in the gunfire exchange. Both involved vehicles were fully occupied, but no physical descriptions of offenders were provided. Suspects were tracked through the identification and gang affiliation of the fatally shot passengers of both vehicles," Jack said to Junior, seeing a hopefully winnable defense.

"What about fingerprints and ownership of the vehicles and weapons recovered at the scene?" Junior asked his father.

"Ownership of vehicles may provide a lead, but it is not conclusive of criminal presence at the scene, nor would be ownership of weapons if any could be provided. Most gangbangers' weapons are untraceable anyway."

Jack, Jr., interrupted, "What if you win this case? Won't you be putting gangbangers back on the street to create more deadly violence? Doesn't it bother you to know that?"

It was disturbing to Jack that his soon-to-be-practicing lawyer son did not understand his role as a defense attorney.

"What do you think we're doing here, Junior? Do you really think that we are allowing more criminal behavior when we hold the prosecutors to prove their cases beyond a reasonable doubt? Do you not realize that we are protecting the arrest and prosecutorial process itself when we fight for the rights of the accused? Wake up! You have a job to do, Son, so do it!

Win or lose but do your job well!"

It was understandable if Ambrose or Amanda would ask that question, as so many good citizens have asked Jack over his years of practice. But Junior was already committed to his profession and needed to put his naiveté behind him, especially if he expected to join his father's firm.

———∿∿———

Another case came in. It was a DUI. A friend had consumed a little too much at a cocktail party fundraiser. It wasn't complicated. It was a "bread-and-butter" typical case of a criminal law practice. Being that people of any walk of life can pick up a DUI, it did not have the stigma of a criminal case, except to the teetotalers of the world or when there was a resulting accident with serious consequences.

"I will guide you on this one, Junior. You will handle it alone with my supervision. Do your best and bring your strategy to me before you go to court," Jack advised with hopeful pride that Junior would get things right. "Thanks, Dad, I won't let you down," Junior said, beaming with hopeful pride in acceptance of the challenge.

Some consequences of DUIs are seen to be more emotionally than legally serious. Families are often seen ripped apart by the toll of alcohol and drug addiction. Alcohol and drugs so often lead to loss of employment and abusive behavior that ruins a once-loving relationship. Jack learned the roles of lawyers and courts to encourage intervention and treatment to correct indulgent behavior before it leads to those serious consequences.

One such case was with a client Jack remembered who could not even attend early morning court without first becoming intoxicated. It was a simple, first-offense DUI with nothing unusual but the blood/alcohol of the defendant being three times the legal limit. A required evaluation returned a treatment recommendation that allowed Jack to reach a plea agreement that would be a non-conviction deferred judgment with treatment conditions. On each of several court appearances, Jack's client could not even stand straight nor speak clearly before the judge to enter the plea and agreed sentence. The client could not even start his day before first getting drunk. He was a functional alcoholic who was somehow able to get through his daily living in a drunken stupor.

Another sad case Jack remembered involved a client who got drunk at home and an accident occurred where his large dog jumped onto a glass coffee table, injuring himself. The client had no other choice but to drive his injured dog to a veterinarian hospital. Veering off the road and hitting a tree sent his poor dog through the windshield, killing him. It was a memorable case that illustrated the unexpected serious consequences of becoming voluntarily incapacitated, even at home, unable to respond to help yourself or others in an emergency.

———

Amanda had finished her interviews and research concerning her assignment in the Juan Pablo Jiménez case. She gathered with her father and brother to discuss her findings.

"Your client here is no saint, but he has matured and changed his ways over the years. He has tried to stay straight and works hard to support his wife and children, along with other family members who live with them. He has been clearly a victim of violence so many times over these past recent years, twice by the same gangbanger who confronted him in this case. He pulled his gun when he saw the offender approach with a gun in hand. Shots were exchanged immediately. It cannot be definitively shown who shot first. But our client's intent was to defend himself from another attack. This time our client got the best of the confrontation.

"I've come to empathize with Juan Pablo, his parentless childhood and street influences that led him astray in his early teens. He was given opportunities that he could not fulfill due to his language barrier and attention deficit disorder that his grandparents who raised him thought to be a mental disability. They have medical opinion to support his ADHD; he was vulnerable and gullible.

"His early peers were street urchins. They stole from fruit and vegetable vendors. They painted symbols on walls that meant little to him. They harassed other kids to join them to pursue their mischievous lifestyle. Older gang members recruited the young to do their violent bidding. Those people became a welcoming family to Juan Pablo, a group that solicited his membership to do unspeakable things. It was a group that dragged Juan Pablo down to their level of unsociable and criminal behavior. When he found his way with maturity to leave his regrettable lifestyle, he worked hard to make amends and create a new life for his budding new family.

"Juan Pablo not only has left the gangs of his past so long ago, but he also mentors community youth at the YMCA to pursue Christian life. He is practicing what he preaches by organizing food drives and clothing drives for the underprivileged poor. He is continually invited to speak about the evils of gangland violence and has condemned the easy accessibility of guns and paraphernalia of war on Chicago streets.

"Juan Pablo Jiménez is not the same person he unfortunately was groomed to be. His maturity enlightened him to be the good person he became, despite his life's adversities. I like him, and I think a jury would too."

Amanda was moved to tears just by her telling what she'd discovered about their client. Her emotions were stirred as would anyone else's upon hearing Juan Pablo's life story.

Jack knew Amanda enjoyed her role in gathering information to help her father's case. He was proud to provide her with encouragement to consider practicing law with him and hopefully show her how justice can prevail. Jack asked Ambrose to join him and his siblings to make this case a family learning experience. Even his wife, Elizabeth, hung around to observe the ongoing preparation of a case that would surely go to trial. Jack planned an exciting and moving defense of Juan Pablo Jiménez. It would demonstrate the true art of a law practice, the art of persuasion to achieve individual justice—justice that cannot be lumped together with all situations that are regulated with rigid black-and-white laws and rules. Individual justice can demonstrate the grey areas of law that allow compassion and understanding to bring a just result. It is referred to by practicing lawyers as "jury nullification"—a verdict that overlooks what may be technically illegal acts to vindicate those who have understandably violated the law.

Chapter 19

Burden of Proof

Discovery materials were exchanged in the Juan Pablo Jiménez case and a future date was set for a jury trial. A bench trial was ready to proceed in the case of DeShawn Robinson and was rushed to trial before other defendants or witnesses would be discovered or come forward to add incriminating evidence against Robinson. Jack filed a "speedy trial" demand with the court.

The bench trial began. The state prosecutor, Lloyd Phillips, gave his opening statement to the judge as to the evidence that would be presented to convict DeShawn Robinson of murder. In a most unusual manner, Jack Keegan waived his opening remarks to allow the case to proceed immediately. Keegan was ready to hold the prosecution to his burden to prove the state's case beyond a reasonable doubt. A more unpredictable jury trial was not demanded being that Jack's argument was based on law and that a judge alone was more certain to find the evidence to be insufficient against Robinson.

The Robinson trial was the shortest murder case that Keegan ever tried. Lloyd Phillips was one of the more seasoned prosecutors, who realized weaknesses in his case but had to pursue a murder conviction without compromise. The trial began.

Assistant State's Attorney (DA) Lloyd Phillips began his opening statement to the presiding judge to enlighten her as to what evidence she could expect to hear in the prosecution of DeShawn Robinson.

"Your Honor, Judge Lorraine McMahon, you will hear testimony from several eyewitnesses who saw two vehicles exchange gunfire on the Eisenhower Expressway, gunfire that left three dead, two in one vehicle and one in the other. Identification of the deceased revealed their membership in two rival street gangs. One of the two recovered vehicles is registered to the defendant, and his fingerprints and DNA were identified throughout his vehicle and on one of the guns used in the murders. Identifiers of other offenders have led us in pursuit to no avail at this time. It is the defendant's speedy trial demand that has prompted his trial before we have completed our case with the arrest of those suspects. With leave of court, we will proceed."

"Very well, Mr. Phillips, thank you. Mr. Keegan, do you have an opening statement you would like to make to the court?" Judge McMahon asked.

"No, Your Honor. We waive opening," answered Keegan.

"You may proceed, Mr. Phillips. Call your first witness."

Witnesses were called to prove the premises of the State's case, and Keegan cross-examined the testimony to reveal no proof of the defendant's presence at the scene of the crime and multiple fingerprints on the recovered guns and throughout both vehicles. The prosecution rested its case, as did the defense without calling a single witness.

Prosecutor Phillips argued the evidence that he put into the record to support what he intended to prove, as outlined in his opening statement. Defense Attorney Keegan highlighted the deficiency of the prosecution's case:

"Your Honor, Judge McMahon, we concede that the State proved what they set out to prove, but their evidence presented falls short of proving their case. The following facts have been established:

1. There was an involved vehicle identified to be registered to Mr. Robinson with his vehicle loaded with his fingerprints among fingerprints of other persons who have not been located.

2. A deceased body with fatal gunshot wounds and a firearm were also found in Mr. Robinson's vehicle. Mr. Robinson's fingerprints, among prints of other persons, were also on the firearm that was shown to have caused the deaths of two occupants in the second involved vehicle.

3. No witness nor other evidence proves Mr. Robinson was present to commit the crime alleged. Fingerprints of a vehicle owner are expected to be found in that vehicle. Fingerprints of many others were also found in the vehicle. Fingerprints of my client, where those of many

individuals are found on that same weapon, prove only that Mr. Robinson handled that weapon at some time but does not prove he handled it at the time of the shooting or that he ever shot the weapon at any time.

4. Prosecution attempts to prove suspected gang affiliation rivalry as a motive to murder is mere conjecture, and without testimony or other direct evidence does not provide sufficient evidence to prove the defendant guilty of murder.

A defense motion for a finding of "not guilty" was sustained. It was another victory for Keegan.

Keegan's victory called for a gathering of friends and prosecutors that Jack had known and battled with for years. It was a congenial celebration of their work together, especially following a case that was so relatively stress-free, such as DeShawn Robinson's case. They would gather at "Jean's," a regular tavern across from the Cook County Criminal Courthouse where lawyers would congregate following trials. No invitations were required. It was a regular spot to meet. Lawyers would come to rejoice or complain about results in their cases.

All had stories of what could have been or should have been. Some shared stories of misery but mostly of humor as they raised their glasses to toast another day. Jack threw his arm around Lloyd—or "Larry" as he liked to be called.

"You have been at this prosecution gig too long, Larry," Jack said to him privately. "Why don't you leave the side of the angels and join us keeping the criminals coming through your revolving door? We'd love to see your grumpy face on our side of the profession. You'd have a good time and make a lot   more money. You know justice can be served on both sides, right?"

"I'm comfortable here, Jack. I have a family and can't risk leaving a regular paycheck," Lloyd answered in an all too often refrain heard from lifelong prosecutors. It was a prosecutor's stock answer to being nudged out of a position that was universally thought to be an internship before entering a professional law practice. Although, prosecutors really believed that they were serving the angels in a society ravaged with criminals and their defense lawyer champions. It would not be a morally rewarding profession for them to enjoy.

All nudging and commentary aside, they were friends and enjoyed each other's company. Another glass was raised for another toast—to what? To anything, it didn't matter. It was a relaxing time at Jean's.

It was always time to pause between trials; whether they were long or short pauses, there had to be a reprieve. It was time for a family vacation. It could not be for too long, though. Criminal law practitioners always must be able to receive calls and be ready on a moment's notice to appear in court. Regular caseloads too had to be tended to, unless there was an associate left behind to manage the store, so to speak. Jack thought about it but could not saddle Junior with the task. Besides, Junior had to be with him and the family. He made arrangements with a competitive colleague to cover.

Skiing was still in season, and there was good powder in Vail. Jack and his family hopped a plane ride to their winter home, where their skiing equipment was anxiously waiting for them to pound the slopes. It was a good time. They enjoyed evenings outdoors around a firepit drinking hot apple cider and hot toddies. Roasting marshmallows and singing old campfire songs added even more to their family enjoyment.

Five days later there was a situation back home that Jack had to handle. His wife and kids, adults but kids to him, nonetheless would stay back in the lodge to finish their vacation.

AUSA Gatlin Driscoll called Keegan to inform him that the bodies of DEA Agent Ford Wilson and DEA Agent Angel Gonzales washed ashore along Biscayne Bay. They needed to locate Elrod Moses for questioning. Keegan could not be helpful. He last saw Moses when his case was dismissed in federal court. He certainly would not inquire of others as to his whereabouts. Keegan had expected the worst for Moses when they last parted ways. He had to be home, though, to keep a lid on things. Jack knew nothing and wanted to know even less. It was even more important that his family was not nearby during a time that unwanted visitors might come around.

Keegan was asked to come in to see Driscoll. Jack had no other cases then pending in Miami but hopped a plane just to keep the appointment with Driscoll. A chair was pulled uncomfortably far from Driscoll's desk, where Jack was asked to sit. Jack knew it would be an uncomfortable conversation. The positioning of the chair alone would give Driscoll a better vantage to review Keegan's body language during questioning. It was an old reliable tactic during interrogations. Jack Keegan could not be so easily intimidated, however. He was often the interviewer, never the interviewee, in cross-examination that would bring discomfort to a testifying witness.

"Where is Raphael Martinez, Mr. Keegan?" AUSA Driscoll asked out of the blue.

Jack's face turned flush in a way Jack always saw as a weakness of his ethnicity, being Irish with pale white skin. It was evidently so noticeable that Driscoll asked Jack if he was all right or needed a glass of water.

"I'm fine, Mr. Driscoll, just fine, and I have not been in touch with Martinez either. Why do you ask?" Keegan answered.

"I have been going over Southern District of Miami cases and found very similar patterns of disappearing witnesses. You will recall Judge

Baldwin's comments following dismissal of the Elrod Moses case. You also represented Raphael Martinez, whose case was dismissed for similar reasons. I certainly hope you are not falling prey to the drug cartel ways of fronting a patsy lawyer to facilitate their bidding. It won't end well for you if you are involved in their evil ways of doing business. Either by their hand or ours, you will pay a hefty price," warned a confident Gatlin Driscoll.

"I'm insulted by your accusations, even by you having suspicions. You had better watch what you say. I came here to see you at my expense and to offer my help in any way that I could. That door is now closed to you.

"As we always hear in matters such as this, 'I'll see you in court.' Good-bye, Mr. Driscoll, and may you go to hell while looking forward to a vacation," said Keegan in a twist on a Celtic expression of Irish diplomacy where the saying goes: "Irish diplomacy is the ability to tell a man to go to hell in a way that he will look forward to the trip." Keegan was of an Irish temperament that was anything but diplomatic.

Attorney Art Zimmerman was contacted and informed of Jack's encounter with AUSA

Driscoll. He was given a "heads up" to be aware of accusations that could also come to his doorstep. They enjoyed a dinner at Joe's Stone Crab Restaurant in Miami Beach before Jack returned home to Chicago.

Jack called his wife, Elizabeth, to fill her in on most of the details of his situation. He optimistically but guardingly warned of safety concerns for her and their family.

"Stay there with the kids for a while longer until everything   settles down. I'm looking every which way and over my shoulder to see what's coming. Please do the same there and stay for as long as you can. If you feel better somewhere else, don't hesitate to go there. Keep in touch, sweetheart. Love to you and the kids."

But things didn't settle down. More bodies floated up to the Bay shoreline. They were Sebastian Fuentes and Emilio Ramos. They were the introducers of Santiago De la Cruz— the third buyer who came to the third drug purchase from Elrod Moses. Gatlin Driscoll put a tail on Keegan. Keegan might lead them to clear this up, Driscoll thought.

Chapter 20

Catching Up with an Old Friend

It was late afternoon one day when a retired old friend from Keegan's years as a Chicago police officer called to invite him out for a drink and to reminisce about old times. His name was Sal Amato. It was good to hear from a friend of simpler times. They met at Jack's home in Chicago. Jack's family was still in Vail, or wherever Elizabeth thought it to be safe for her family.

"What's going on with you and your family, Sal?" Jack asked with the answer not expected.

"We renewed our vows of marriage last November, Jack. We are doing well, and our kids are grown and on their own," Sal answered.

"And what of your 'gumad'?" Jack asked. "How is she doing?"

"I have another, Jack, and she is FINE! She knows how and when to light my fire, Jack. She is a good girl!"

Girl? Jack thought, knowing Sal had to be three times her age to even call her a girl, but Jack would not make him uncomfortable or allow him to gloat by asking her age.

"Do you ever stop back at the Hidden Cove or Reggie's across from the 20th District station?" Sal asked.

"Are those places still there?" Jack questioned, barely remembering the old police hangouts after work where they could drink watered-down booze for free.

"No, Sal, I have been traveling in different circles since those old days. But we had a lot of fun, didn't we?"

"And women, Jack! Don't forget all those young 'braciola' we met and devoured after work—and sometimes during work—over the years past. What a great job we had and what good times we enjoyed back then." J a c k remembered those good times as a distant memory of his youthful past but then realized how Sal was still reliving that time as his life-long accomplishment. It was good to see him again and remember those times, as it was good to remember life experiences with those who had passed away. Jack was happy to be moving forward in his life with new activities and adventures that were equally, if not more, fulfilling.

They continued to joke and banter about their past experiences together on the "job"—a label which all police officers use when talking about police work. They even paused to re-member those officers who didn't make it be-cause they were killed—or indicted! It was a time now thought of fondly by Jack, but not all consuming as it was for Sal.

They promised to get together again, but that would not happen.

Jack was homesick for his family to return. He reached out to Elizabeth to check on her and the kids.

"Hi, sweetheart; how are you and the kids doing? I think you all can return home soon. I just want to be sure it is still safe here. It won't be long," Jack said, being lonely but careful for his treasured family.

A call came in to Keegan from Raphael Martinez. "I got picked up here in Chicago for questioning about a case in Florida. Do I need you for this?" Martinez asked.

Keegan interrupted, "AUSA Gatlin Driscoll is suggesting that you—and even I—may have something to do with witnesses disappearing in his cases. He is an asshole, and I strongly suggest that you don't talk to him or anyone else about anything, not even to me. I don't know anything and don't want to know. I can advise you only to keep your mouth shut. You should also be aware that you may be under surveillance and all your conversations may be recorded. I wouldn't be surprised if mine were too. So, hang in there and resist any temptation to cooperate with that son-of-a-bitch. Be aware that his snooping may also cause snooping by the cartels. So be alert and speak to no one."

"Understood, Boss!"

"And don't call me 'Boss.' I know you are using it merely as an expression of familiarity, but

I wouldn't want it to be taken the wrong way. Okay?"

"Okay, Mr. Keegan," Raphael said with a chuckle, knowing full well how to keep his cool and his mouth shut. He believed and probably could handle this kind of pressure better than Keegan—or anyone for that matter.

Driscoll turned up the heat to find Elrod Moses. There would be no giving up in his pursuit. He was to be relentless, as were all federal prosecutors. Keegan thought he had put Miami and all its heat behind him. But even in Chicago, things were not nearly ready to cool. Jack told his family to stay away longer and have fun.

Chapter 21

Fearing the Cartels and Teaching the Family Practice

Jack had to know what happened to Santiago De la Cruz. Why would Moses confess to having the drugs and money if Cruz was able to slip away from the bust? He wanted to know but would not dare ask if Martinez paid Moses and Lopez a visit and took the money and product. If Martinez did, then the money would already be laundered, and the product would have been distributed. If he didn't find anything, Moses and Lopez would have stashed everything somewhere else, or otherwise Moses lied, and Cruz really took everything with him. Maybe Martinez never took care of loose ends, and Moses took off with Lopez and the stash, and they are still on the run. The cartels would surely catch up with them.

Overthinking the alternate possible events frightened Keegan even more.

In further thought, what could he do with the information? It is what it is. Nothing can change anything. You know what they say about curiosity, and Keegan did not want to be the cause of that likely outcome.

Jack had to get back to work and helplessly let the investigation take its course. He knew that he would be one of the first to know if anything develops. He also knew that his family could not be left in exile. He would still, however, be looking over his shoulder all the time.

The trial date for the Jiménez case was nearing. Jack prepared his son to co-chair the trial with him. He was to have Junior prepare and present the opening argument, but the closing was to be Jack's alone. The closing argument had to be extraordinarily persuasive to encourage the jury to vindicate his client. It was a risky defense to seek jury nullification of statutorily specific crimes. It was a fallback defense that Jack remembered from his school days' professor in criminal law. Fairness and compassion would have to be evoked to bring a successful verdict.

Being that Amanda was brought to tears when learning of Juan Pablo's life story, her father asked her to prepare the closing argument that he would deliver to the jury. She would do best to bring out the fairness and compassion of the jury.

"Hear ye, hear ye, hear ye," the bailiff announced. "The court calls to be heard the case of People v. Juan Pablo Jiménez, The Honorable Judge Lincoln Davis presiding."

Assistant State's Attorney (DA) Robert Cassidy began his very predictable prosecution with no surprises. He was straightforward in his opening statement to the jury that they would hear of a Mexican standoff without the standoff in that both men were seen drawing guns on each other and almost immediately began shooting. He would offer into evidence a confession translated from Spanish to English where Jiménez admitted that he drew his gun and shot first, initiating an exchange of gunfire with multiple shots from each subject. Forensic evidence would be introduced to prove that the fatal shooting of nine-year-old Isabella Morales as well as the other victim participating in the shootout was from the defendant's gun and from his firing direction to both victims. It would also be proved that the defendant was carrying his weapon illegally.

Jack Keegan, Jr., assistant to Jack Keegan, Sr., began his opening statement to the jury on behalf of Juan Pablo Jiménez. It was a masterfully done joint effort by both Amanda and Junior that would tell their client's life story that the jury would later hear from the defendant himself when he would take the stand to testify. It was a risky promise in that if the trial, as it progressed, should later call for a change of strategy where their client would be ill advised to testify, the jury would hold the promise of untold testimony against him in their deliberations. It was promised, nonetheless. It was an important defense strategy.

The prosecution went forward to introduce evidence that would convict Juan Pablo Jiménez of murder should there be no compelling defense evidence that would rebut the State's case. There was only one witness who could persuade the jury to acquit the defendant—the defendant himself.

The defendant was called to the stand to testify and, through a court interpreter for language translation, was sworn in. Jack Keegan directed the defendant's testimony with a translator providing his answers in English.

"State your name, sir."

"Juan Pablo Jiménez."

"Are you a citizen of the United States?"

"Yes, I was born here."

"And yet your native language is Spanish?"

"Yes, I was raised by my Mexican grandparents who did not speak English. I was never schooled in English."

"And where were you schooled?"

"Mostly by my grandmother at home. I wasn't accepted well in school."

"Why was that?"

"I was a troublemaker."

"And how much trouble did you make?"

"A lot of trouble, and crimes; I was a bad kid and hung around with many other bad kids.

I lived mostly on the streets, committing a lot of crimes. I was arrested many times and was sent to juvenile homes and jails when I got older."

"Did you see a doctor back then?"

"Yes, for a mental disability. I had ADHD and other things like that. I took pills for a while."

"Are your grandparents still alive?"

"No. They died when I was very young."

"Where did you live?"

"As I said, I lived mostly on the streets, or in jail."

"And who helped you get by in life? How did you make money to live?"

"Other kids had me help them commit crimes and gave me some money to live on."

"What kind of crimes did they have you do?"

"All kinds; I did time for robbery, car jackings, and murder. As I got older, I changed my ways and left those people behind me. I saw that they were using me and pretending to care about me. They were not the family I needed."

"And what have you done since then?"

"I found hard work, it's a good job paying wages that get me by. I picked up another one for extra income. They keep me busy but don't interfere with my food and clothing drives that I run in my old neighborhood."

"You do charity work and hold two jobs?"

"Yes, I do. And I have a wife and two kids who I love very much. They are my family—a family that I made myself, one that I never had."

"And you also—"

"I also joined the YMCA to teach kids to be good and live a Christian life of prayer and good works."

"Have you been invited to speak to groups to guide others to do good and condemn your past life of crime?"

"I have and continue to be invited to speak to many youths, and I always condemn my past bad behavior as hurtful not only to others, but also to yourself. I always tell how sad and regretful my past life was and how full of grace and joy I feel today. It seems to work. Kids change when they hear those things. They feel the love in the room when I tell them. I do love them."

———～～～———

"Now tell me what happened that brings you to court today."

"I was leaving my work at the store when I noticed a man that had robbed and beat me twice before approach with a gun in his hand. I was also carrying a gun because I have been robbed many other times besides by him and needed it for self-defense. This case happened so fast because I knew what to expect from him and had to shoot first. He was pointing his gun right at me when he approached. I don't support gun possession at any time, but guns are everywhere. I would have been carrying the gun legally if I did not have a criminal background. It was only for self-defense. I'm so sorry this happened, but I believe I wouldn't be alive to be telling you this if I did not do what I did. I wish this didn't happen, and I am so sorry for the death of the young girl. It will haunt me forever. I would never want this to happen to anyone. I regularly condemn easy access to guns and gang violence when I speak to community groups."

After a short cross-examination that included the defendant's criminal history that the defendant already admitted, the parties rested their cases for arguments that were also short. A.S.A. Robert Cassidy repeated what he'd promised in opening and delivered into evidence. Jack Keegan summarized Juan Pablo's story that was left purposely unembellished, so the message and person of Juan Pablo Jiménez continued to resonate clearly with the jury. His words would do more to help him than would Jack Keegan's.

After two hours' deliberation and several moistened handkerchiefs left abandoned on the jury-room table, Juan Pablo Jiménez was acquitted with a unanimous verdict of "Not Guilty." It was unknown if the jury agreed with what the defendant claimed to be preemptive self-defense, or just jury nullification of a charge that would not set well with the jury to convict him of murder. In any case, it was a just result for a reformed man with a sad story. It was true justice. Even the deceased nine-year-old girl would agree, God bless her, Keegan thought.

———

That case brought more joy to Jack than any other in his long career. He took on more and more "pro bono" cases that he could see warranted for special consideration, cases that public defenders would often neglect. He warned his children not to be consumed by money-grabbing income for their legal services. He promised they would lose the joy of being a lawyer if they did. There is no greater satisfaction to a lawyer than winning cases that bring just results. That's what we're here to do—serve justice.

He also warned his children about money-grabbing corruption in the courts that would prevent justice. There were things his children had to learn that would never be taught in law school. They were to be made aware of judges and court personnel to avoid when possible. They had to keep their eyes and ears open, and their mouths shut, as Jack learned so long ago as a police officer.

"Your objective as a lawyer is to win your case on the merits of good argument. Avoid anyone who gets in your way of that, but don't try to change the world to get rid of corruption. If you do try, you will be fighting the scorn of every court you set foot into. Your crusade will get in the way of your objectives.

"Choose your forum, if you can, and give your case your best argument to win. That's it. That's how it works," Jack preached all-knowingly to give the best guidance he could.

"Always learn your surroundings. Be aware. Use common sense."

As a proud and gloating father would do, Jack took his kids around to the various courts to meet and greet the best of the best people he knew and worked with. He gave Jack, Jr., the lead in every case that came in but always stood by to counsel him when needed. Amanda came too when she could. She was excited by her newfound waiting career opportunity. Amanda realized that she'd never paid much attention to her father's work. She never before appreciated his social contribution as she did then.

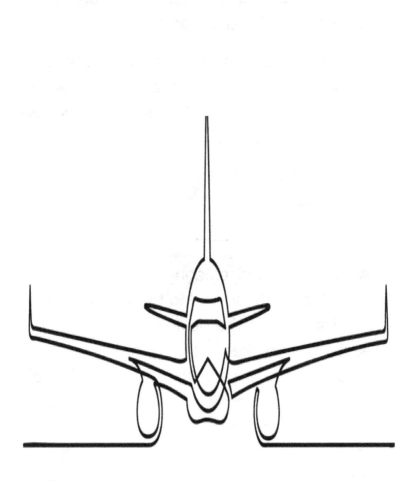

Chapter 22

Back to Miami to Clean Up Loose Ends

J ack comforted himself that things were back to good, with all loose ends tied up with his Miami clientele. He still wondered about the whereabouts or fate of Santiago De la Cruz, but he tried to put that issue out of his mind. Then Raphael Martinez called again. Fear for the worst returned.

"When we last talked, Jack, you warned me to keep quiet about everything. I know you don't want to hear anything that could put you in the middle of something, but I must tell you that nothing happened between me and Elrod. I paid him a visit to clear up our problem, but nobody and nothing were there—no Moses, no Lopez, no product, and no cash. Sorry I didn't let you know, but I didn't think you wanted to know."

Fear consumed Jack. Things were still

unsettled. He had to clean things up for his and his family's safety. There could be no loose ends. He slammed the door shut on Driscoll, who would have done nothing for him anyway. Jack turned again to Agent Ariana De Leon and regrettably had to distance himself again from his family for their safety. He swore to himself that he would not again get involved with the deadly game of drug trafficking. Jack should have listened to his father years ago.

Jack had to turn to a friend who he knew could clear up the mess that his client, Elrod Moses, got him into. Ariana De Leon—a trusted and capable friend who would be fearless enough to do what-ever it took to do the job. She also had the needed resources at her disposal. Keegan called to meet with Ariana. They met in her Miami office.

"Ariana, I'm in a jam through no fault of my own. I need help and have no one to turn to. I know things will not end well if I don't clear things up. I must know, and I'm sure you would like to know, how things ended with Elrod Moses and Santiago De la Cruz. The U.S. Attorney's Office and per-haps two cartels are breathing down my neck. I will do whatever I can to help you help me. Please bring me back into your confidence and know that

I will work with you discreetly."

It hit Keegan to realize that he was offering to become like one of his own informants that he groomed, and that little or no benefit came their way. In fact, Jack knew, many informants lost everything by undertaking cooperation agreements that led to a tortuous death. But he also knew that he had no choice. He could not do it alone.

"All right, Jack, I will have your 'six' on this and put you back in the field. We believe De la Cruz is back in Mexico doing well and is a rising star in cartel land. We have no information on Moses. We think he might be dead or will be soon if he surfaces. Same with Lopez. It will be your mission, if you decide to accept it, to go to Mexico and find out," said Ariana in her rare and subtle humor, referencing it to be an "impossible mission."

Keegan knew the risks but felt safe with Ariana and her team, perhaps as his informants felt with him as they accepted their undercover missions. He went back to Miami for briefing.

His Chicago office was still operational in his absence with his son having passed the bar exam and completing his assigned DUI case without a problem. Jack recommended that he counsel with an old Chicago friend and colleague, Edward Konicki, if he had any questions on cases that came up while he was gone. He gave his son and his family contact information if anything of concern arose.

"I'm proud of you, Jack," said Jack, Sr., no longer calling him "Junior." He was proud that his son would someday be a partner in the firm of Keegan and Keegan. Perhaps it would be Keegan, Keegan, and Keegan if Amanda joined the family business.

"Love to you all. I hope to be back home soon," said Jack.

Keegan thought he would set up shop with, but was not well received by, Miami attorney Art Zimmerman, who somehow knew the heat that Jack felt in his lingering Miami matters. Zimmerman told Keegan that he would have to re-open a Miami office, if needed. There was no room in Zimmerman's firm, even for temporary use. Zimmerman's rejection gave Jack considerable pause for concern. Being Keegan's Miami mentor and all-knowing of things, if Zimmerman was worried about being too close to Keegan, then Jack's worries were certainly not unfounded.

Before setting out on his mission, Keegan got a call from someone who remained nameless but who expressed his concern about Moses.

"We heard of your success in getting our man's case dismissed, but we have not heard from him. We are concerned. Perhaps we can meet to discuss what you know about his whereabouts," said the caller from a telephone number traced back to Mendez territory in Mexico.

"I'll get back to you on that. Where can I reach you?" said Keegan while knowing no contact information would be provided.

"No need," said the caller. "We'll get back to you soon."

Jack immediately let Ariana know of the call, but she already knew, being that Jack's phone had already been tapped to gather needed information. He should have known that it was tapped. That's how things worked.

It was revealing that the Mendez cartel was unaware of the situation with Moses. Ariana and the DEA believed that Mendez was also unaware of De la Cruz and unaware that the Reyes cartel were involved in the sting when Moses was arrested.

Ariana concluded that Mendez did not even know anything about De la Cruz. Mendez must have thought that only drugs were confiscated in the bust, no money, and that the bust of Moses was legit by the two agents named in the report.

The enlightening call led the DEA to focus on Reyes's operations. A mission was put together to saturate Michoacán with agents to find De la Cruz and others who could clear things up. They had to account for two murdered agents and several witnesses, as well as give Keegan his peace of mind. The DEA's best agents were assigned to the task. Agent Greg Forrester, who'd worked with Keegan in Operation Wetsuit, was glad to volunteer. He relished any work that would target cartels. And Greg came to like Jack as well. Jack Keegan was reputed to be a strong asset before, and he would be again.

The mission was planned, and replanned. Ariana could not let this one fail at the expense of Keegan, Forrester, and others she was putting in harm's way. She'd softened since her youthful and aggressive years that passed so quickly by. Ariana often dwelled on past times with Jack in their so-casual relationship that began so awkwardly. She remembered her time with him to have been more satisfying than she'd let on at the time. She was hoping to rekindle the flame of passion, but perhaps too many years had passed, and he would probably not feel the same anymore.

Ariana De Leon was still dedicated to her work and would let no sappy emotion get in the way of duty. She gathered with her team to review mission plans that changed over and over again. The mission would be coded "Operation West Coast." It did not yet meet the approval of her team. The objective, the most important detail, was not entirely in focus.

"What are we truly trying to accomplish here?" Agent Forrester exclaimed.

"Unlike in Operation Wetsuit, we do not have a clear understanding of what we could call a success here. Do we just gather information, or will we set cartels after each other, or will we go on the attack directly? I'm sorry, Agent De Leon, but I don't feel confident that we are going about this one correctly. What do you think, Jack?"

"I think we need more information before we go in like storm troopers. Send in someone to do reconnaissance. Find out about De la Cruz and your murdered agents without your activities being discovered. We need someone to work his way into the Reyes cartel. It should be one or two of our agents who are best at assimilating into the group. They of course must be Hispanic and fluent in Spanish as their natural language. We will then be better able to assess our mission objectives," Keegan asserted, suddenly confident that he had the obvious answer that could solve his problems.

"Of course," said Ariana. "We all know that we need more information. The question remains: 'How far away will we all be to support our infiltrating agents if trouble should arise?' And what are we to do then if they need us? How do we save them and our mission?"

Ariana was right. She needed to protect her agents and was reluctant to expose them to the tortuous harm they would encounter if they were discovered. They all thought that way. They were all skittish, to say the least. They had to bring another approach to the mission. Jack thought of another idea.

"You all must remember my police days' informant who I brought to our last mission, Raphael Martinez. I have since represented him in another case he picked up. He now considers me to be

a friend, and I must say I have gotten to appreciate his association with me now more than ever
before. He may be useful again here. I can ask if
he will help, but he will expect more than a 'thank
you' from us. He works for big cash money only
now. But he is good at what he does, is well known
in cartel land, and is as ruthless as they come.
Perfect for the assignment."

Ariana thought pensively and nodded repeatedly of her approval of Jack's suggestion. Raphael
was to become a paid mercenary, a disposable
agent of war.

"Agreed?" Ariana asked of her group.

"Agreed!" the group answered in unison. The
challenge was left to bring Raphael aboard. Jack
reached out to him.

Raphael was to meet up with Jack at Joe's
Restaurant in Miami Beach—a place so unsuit-
able for Raphael's attire, but suitable as a makeshift office for Jack's purpose. Raphael ordered a
hamburger being that he was unfamiliar with the
restaurant specialty.

Keegan was surprised to hear that Raphael
had already hooked up with the Reyes cartel but

was still doing business with Mendez. Jack was even more surprised that he agreed to help in the mission for no compensation, considering it to be a favor for a close friend. But even then, with Raphael's extended hand of friendship, Jack's feelings would never be reciprocal. It was all business with Jack.

Raphael also had his own business motives for his cooperation anyway. He saw his mission not to be as risky as it was to be an opportunity to advance his position in cartel operations. He could take advantage of any discovered rivalry weakness in either of the two competing cartels targeted by Jack's group. It could strengthen his drug-trafficking career. He was not afraid of the challenge.

Raphael Martinez's business motives were always recognized by Keegan to be in service to his entrepreneurial ambitions. Every criminal case of Raphael that Keegan was retained to handle became more and more serious and complex as years went by. He was always an opportunist in his trade. He was smarter than most of his competitors—and law enforcement.

Ariana's team members were relieved to be

adding Raphael to their group to do the dirty work, especially the Hispanic group members who were fearful for their safety. It was a very dangerous assignment for the infiltrator. The agents were to let Raphael discover what was going on, and they would mostly lend support from a distance. Plans were coming together.

"We best send Raphael Martinez in alone, without our support being as close behind as we expected it to be provided for our agents," Ariana told the group. "It may prove to be safer for him as well, being that everyone in cartel land is so on edge with all the recent activities. We will strategically saturate the Michoacán, Reyes's areas of operation where we expect that De la Cruz may be found, and the Mendez headquarters' areas in Veracruz and nearby Puebla. Martinez will find out what's going on before we make our next move."

Martinez was making his own plans. His strategy would be shared with the group only as he saw fit for his own protection. He was going to stay as far away from the group as he could.

Chapter 23

A New Mission in Mexico

Raphael entered the Reyes territory in Michoacán. He was greeted as a rock star by the fellow soldiers transplanted from Mendez territory following the latest shakeup in cartel land. They were unaware that Martinez was working for both the Mendez and now the Reyes cartels, and certainly not aware of his new DEA mission. They greeted him by the same name they use for all their compatriots. When speaking English, all greetings were preceded with "Bro." In Spanish it was "Hermano."

"Hermano! Que Pasa, El?" Raphael was greeted by the crew. "All good, bro. Et tu?" El answered.

"I'm looking to drum up some new business, a new distribution route. Who should I talk to for that?" El asked.

"Talk to Cruz," said one of the crew who stepped forward to introduce El to those of the crew who did not know Raphael, or at least well enough to trust him with the information. "He cool, bros," said Tito, a soldier compadre from Raphael's Miami pickup and distribution days.

"Santiago De la Cruz?" El questioned of the "Teat," as Tito was affectionately or teasingly called, being that he was very heavy chested.

"What's he doing now back here? I thought he was still in Miami."

"He got bumped up to boss around here after his last deal back there," Tito told El. "I can let him know you want to see him   if you want."

"No thanks, Teat, I'm sticking around a while. I'm sure I will run into him. Things are drying up a little back home, and I thought a little more work could keep me busy. No big deal."

It was important to report back to Keegan,

who was Raphael's only contact as Ariana De Leon agreed he would be. El would use a cheap throwaway phone to talk with Keegan in code. It was safer than the high-tech encrypted government-issue phones that would prompt his demise if discovered. Besides, throwaway phones were always used in the drug-trafficking trade.

Jack Keegan was still in Miami, where it would not be suspect if he received a call from his past client. The substance of the call had to be vague but communicative that Cruz was there, operational, and promoted. The call was received and understood.

More information was needed to clarify mission objectives. Cruz was alive and doing well, which put a lot of the mission in better focus, but the whereabouts and/or fate of others was equally important to know. Martinez had to keep digging. Everyone else was staying away to give him operational space.

Days went by with Raphael making himself comfortable with Tito and the crew, reminiscing about old times and how much better things used to be back then. El knew that it would make others suspicious if he were in too much of a hurry to ask questions about their business and business associates. He just hung out with the guys for a while. It broke the ice.

Moses appeared, seemingly from nowhere, to greet Raphael with caution while remembering his last conversation with him and Jack Keegan at the shores of Biscayne Bay. Moses got right to the point.

"Why are you here, you motherfucker? You lost?" Moses said in a cautionary but confrontational way.

"Last time I saw you, you were going to take a piece of me. Why? What did I ever do to you?" Moses continued.

"No, you lied to our friend and lawyer, Jack Keegan. He did not deserve you to be ungrateful for all he did to save your black ass. I was there to save him from your stupidity, El," said Raphael, calling Elrod by Raphael's own nickname. "Things have settled back down since then. Let's put it behind us, El."

There was no love lost between them, but

Moses and Raphael agreed to work together again under Cruz. Cruz would make himself known to Raphael after considering the rift between Rafael and Moses. Cruz was amused by it all. Santiago De la Cruz introduced himself to Raphael Martinez. He brought Raphael an irresistible offer to develop his own transportation line from Michoacán to Chicago, with alternate transportation through Miami, but only on the condition that Raphael get rid of Moses and accept Manuel Lopez as his associate. Moses was no longer useful being that he made himself a target following the Miami deal. It was a "no-brainer." Raphael was to move up in his trade. But what would he tell the DEA? He couldn't betray his friend Jack Keegan, but he couldn't resist the offer either.

Raphael became comfortable enough to ask Cruz about the "deal gone bad" in Miami with Moses. Cruz did not hesitate to tell of the stupidity that Moses showed to jeopardize an otherwise winnable deal.

"All Moses had to do was to roll with the punches. He was to be arrested and charged with only two of three deals and share all proceeds of the third deal that allowed us to retrieve all Reyes money and Mendez product from the transaction. He had to get greedy and dispose of all witnesses and grab the cash and product for himself. Was he nuts? Where would he go to sell the product? Where would he go to launder all that cash? Lopez was gullible to buy into Moses's plan, but Lopez, unlike Moses, has potential. He will be a good mule for us. Keep him safe and kill that other son-of-a-bitch. Okay? Moses would have been disposed of already, but we needed him to return our assets first."

It was understandable that it was much easier for Moses to bring contraband back to Mexico from the United States than it was to get it to the U.S. from Mexico.

"Okay, boss. I can see why you have gotten as far as you did. Thanks for your confidence. I'll be good for it."

———

Rafael was more hesitant this time to report back on his newfound business friendship. Cruz offered Raphael the chance of a lifetime for wealth, power, and success beyond his expectations. He hesitated but called his friend and lawyer, Jack Keegan.

"Please, Jack, understand that I am in a position that I have always dreamed of. If I accept an offer to move up in my business, I will be set for life. If I refuse, I will be nobody, or worse yet, dead. Maybe I will end up dead anyway, but I always remember the line in the *Godfather* movie where Hyman Roth tells Michael, 'This is the business we have chosen.' It is the best choice that I have, Jack. Help me here, Jack."

Jack advised him to do the right thing, but he knew it was best to have Moses out of the way, especially away from the Mendez cartel. Raphael would confide in Jack and trust that all said would be held confidential. It would be. Jack merely reported back to the team that Moses made it back to deliver the cash and product to Cruz, but having done that he wouldn't be alive for long. He left Lopez out of his report.

The team could not move in quickly enough to save Moses, and why would they? Moses killed their agents and witnesses, and they already had most of the information they needed to know. The team stayed back for Rafael to finish gathering information.

Manuel Lopez was the only link to the demise of all who confided in Moses and allowed his sabotage of their trust. Lopez was lucky to be spared the fate of Moses and of all whom Moses betrayed. Rafael was lucky to have Lopez assigned to work with him. Lopez was the only link left that could account for all that went down—all that Raphael was sent to find out.

Of course, Santiago De la Cruz was the other, more knowledgeable link who put the original deal together. It was a pretty good scheme that Raphael later discovered was the prelude to a takeover of the Mendez cartel. With all loose ends accounted for, the DEA team was able to back off and let things happen.

Keegan felt safer too. Mendez would be busy protecting its territories and distribution routes without bothering to snoop into the affairs of a Miami lawyer and his clients. Jack's work was done. It was time to go home—and never again to Miami.

Raphael stayed in Michoacán for a while learning the ropes of his new position. Jack and he would not talk for a while during Raphael's job transition to become a boss. Things were looking good for all, except for the Mendez cartel.

Chapter 24

A Safe Homecoming

Jack and his family were relieved to be safely back together. Business was doing well with Jack, Jr., at the helm, although he was still learning his way as an intern. Amanda started law school and pestered her father and brother with all kinds of law student questions. Elizabeth was being her best, as she always was, as a loving wife and mother. All was good.

Jack reminisced so lovingly about his wife, Elizabeth. She was always there for Jack, through the not bad, but less than good times. But the good times were great. Elizabeth was a challenge to Jack when first dating so many years ago. She was a social butterfly with a circle of friends that protected her from leaving the group for love or money. He was happy to break through her circle to capture her heart, as she did his.

The Keegan family took a well-deserved vacation the following summer. Jack surprised them with a newly acquired ranch in Colorado. A beautiful, gentleman's barn housed some livestock that were cared for by the neighboring family who lived there full time. Jack knew he would need more horses than the two that came with the property. But it was okay to get used to riding and caring for those before taking on more responsibility. They were city folk, green to the earthy western lifestyle they would come to love.

A small but suitable lake provided a breathtaking view from their kitchen at sunrise. It was a natural watering hole for Jack's livestock. He planned to stock the water with plenty of fish that they could catch and fry at a campfire, or release to swim another day. Jack thought he would learn to strum a guitar to add ambiance to campfire gatherings and sing-alongs. It was his retirement dream home.

For now, he thought, he would provide the guidance necessary for his children to achieve their goals and dreams. "Do what you like, and be good at it," Jack would often say. He would teach them the importance of R & R to follow stressful days of hard work. He would teach them the importance of family closeness, no matter what life experiences come your way. He would teach them to love their life or change it early on. "Don't become bitter about what could have been. Make it happen."

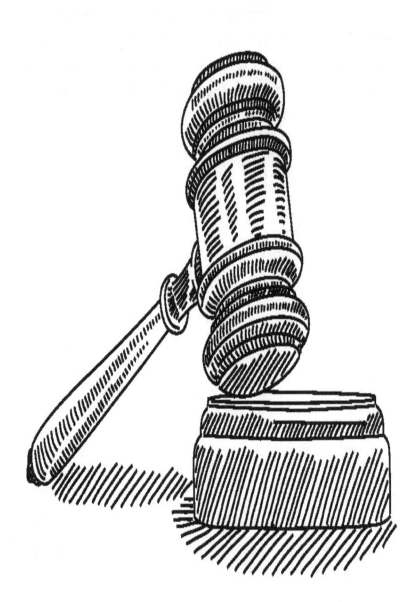

Chapter 25

The Jury Returns a Verdict

Keegan remembered everything that made him who he was—the "good, bad, and ugly" as was once said in a classic Hollywood movie. His life reflected the reality of life, the way things were and the choices that must be made to live it. Jack had his joys and regrets that most remember in their lives, but things were mostly good.

Jack was called back to the courtroom for the reading of the verdict that was reportedly reached by the jury in his latest case with Raphael. His longtime client was already there in custody waiting for Jack's arrival back to court for the jury's decision.

"All rise," the bailiff exclaimed as the jury returned to the court following four long days of lengthy deliberation in the case of People v.

Raphael Martinez. All courtroom eyes were riveted on the blank stares of the jurors as they entered and took their respective seats in the box. At the direction of Presiding Judge Joseph Nichols, the jury foreman stood for the judge's query.

"Mr. Foreman of the jury, have you all reached a verdict?"

"We have, Your Honor."

"What say you."

The jury foreman cleared his throat to deliver the verdict:

"We, the jury in this case, find the defendant, Raphael Martinez, NOT guilty as charged in each and every count of the indictment."

"So say you all?"

In unison, the jurors responded, "We do, Your Honor."

Raphael was released from custody there and then. No returning to his holding cell before being processed out.

Jack Keegan nodded his appreciation to the jury for vindicating his client. Judge Nichols congratulated the jury and both Jeremy Heitkamp for the prosecution and Jack Keegan for the defense for their jobs well done. Jack Keegan smiled and said, "We all do our part to serve justice, Your Honor."

Keegan shuffled his papers to his briefcase as he congratulated Raphael for the successful case outcome. Martinez thanked Keegan for his "fine work" and stood defiantly to court personnel and the gallery as if he was deserving of the vindication.

"Let's stop for a drink to celebrate, Jack," Raphael exclaimed, trying to reignite their relationship that Raphael thought of as friendly.

"Can't now. Catch you next time," Jack retorted, keeping it all business.

Jack Keegan was back to his office catching up on his missed calls and tardy motion filings. He was back to defending his clientele in other cases filling his calendar.

Raphael Martinez continued to do what he always did—what he knew best—dealing, trafficking, and protecting his territory. He had to retake some areas that were lost to rival dealers while he was lying low before trial. When all was running smooth again, he was off to Miami with his new girlfriend for a short respite. Carmen Castro, an attractive Cuban immigrant who'd recently settled in Chicago with her family, was Raphael's latest arm-candy. She and he were meeting up with friends on South Beach. Carmen was so proud to be with Raphael, the big shot of her hood. Before leaving on his trip, Raphael had two Mexican stallions delivered to Jack's newly acquired family ranch in Colorado.

But within a week, things got out of hand back home while Raphael was away. He needed to return earlier than expected. There was full-blown territorial warfare threatening his whole operation. He called Jesse, one of his lieutenant enforcers.

"I want you to get this under control, Jesse. I will be back on the next plane out of here."

"Sure thing, El. I'll try to get everything smooth," Jesse assured.

Within hours, Raphael and Carmen landed back at O'Hare heading towards their car parked in the terminal garage.

"Hold on, El and Miss Fancy Pants. We need to talk," said one of two obvious gangbangers ominously pointing Glocks to their heads.

"Oh, shit!" Raphael exclaimed, knowing his time had come to an end.

Martinez's acquittal was short lived.

Raphael Martinez and his girlfriend were bound and forced into the trunk of his car at gunpoint. The trunk lid was slammed closed upon them, and two ignited railroad flares were flung onto the car's interior seats. As the torched car burned, it was said that wailing screams were heard for several minutes. One could smell the burning flesh in the smoke.

Jack Keegan had just heard that news of his client's torturous death in a local news report shortly before a call came in from the murder suspect—a rival cartel gang member, then being held at Chicago Police Headquarters. Jack was handsomely retained to insulate his new client from a police interrogation and to protect his constitutional rights. Raphael's killer's case would be Jack's last case before retirement and turning his practice over to his new partner, Jack, Jr.; Junior's father would always be close for guidance. If Amanda should later join the firm of Keegan and Keegan, Jack would be proud to see his legacy firm of Keegan, Keegan, and Keegan. Jack knew that Ambrose, however, would always be leading the next popular protest for social justice. It's okay, Jack thought, justice is a good cause to serve.

Keegan was soon leaving his office with briefcase in hand to arrive at CPD headquarters to protect Raphael's killer's rights. "It's time to serve justice again," he reflected. "It's all in the name of justice."

 Epilogue

J ack Keegan was tired of the daily grind these latest years. He was not as enthused to tackle cases as he was before his last case defending Raphael Martinez. He could not reach deep within himself to defend Raphael's killer. His relationship with El and the gruesomeness of his death and his poor companion was stressing his sensibilities to prevent a wholehearted defense. He passed the torch to his son to keep the flame burning bright for justice. Jack and Elizabeth retired to their Colorado ranch and embraced nature at its finest.

Amanda graduated from law school and joined her brother at the firm. Ambrose visited his parents at the ranch more frequently than his siblings, being that they were hard at work fighting cases that came their way. Ambrose's fight for social equities was more sporadic and unorganized, giving him time to cultivate his latest talent as an artist. He also appreciated the ranch more than his siblings and set up an easel to capture its natural beauty.

As Jack reviewed his life to make sense of all that he'd done, he realized the arrogance of mankind to believe that they are more deserving than other creatures to control nature. It is only man who competes with nature in the pretext of improving it. It is only man who kills for purposes other than survival—survival for food and to protect their own. It is only man who doesn't appreciate the natural order of things—the justice of it all, if you will. Nature doesn't waste its own beautifully functional surroundings to "improve" things. Nature doesn't rule creatures and things, except by instinct and godly design.

If man were to properly contribute to nature, man would take measures to preserve what God has intended, preventing natural disasters rather than creating man's own. Man would appreciate the preciousness and beauty of living things. Would man eat his pets for enjoyment of a good meal? Some would, but most wouldn't think of it. Man is the unique species that imposes rules on each other to protect man from his own stupidity and ruthlessness—all in the name of justice, a justice that is so unnecessary in the natural order.

Jack and Elizabeth finally understood what was most important in life, not that they were ungratified by doing what was considered important in a man's life. Their lives changed in retirement, and they knew it was for the better. They had a whole new perspective on things.

The retired Keegans loved living on the ranch. They acquired and cared for all kinds of animals and appreciated Raphael's contribution of their two young stallions. They treasured them and all their animals. They learned to live off the land without grocery shopping. They no longer ate meat from cellophane-covered packages. They no longer ate any meat at all. They became vegetarians, unable to otherwise look their friendly creatures in the eye. They felt good and at peace and being one with nature.

The ranch house was built of logs held solid with mud and straw. It was large across the lake view and with a large wooden deck wrapping three sides. In nice weather seasons, Jack and Elizabeth enjoyed coffee and breakfast on the porch facing east to enjoy the morning sun glimmering on their lake—a view also enjoyed from their kitchen window in cooler weather. In the evening it was a bottle of red wine that was shared on the west porch to welcome the sunset over the always-snowcapped mountains.

They do as most ranchers do in the west: they tap into the nearest aquifer to draw their water. Recent drought conditions caused by climate change have put ample supply in jeopardy, however, but they enjoy what they have for now and hope that people will act to protect our planet for future generations. Jack built a greenhouse to keep fruits and vegetables growing year-round and extended the barn to shelter their outside animals in extremely inclement weather. Jack's treasured Bentley was traded for two reliable pickup trucks that could carry heavy supplies needed occasionally at the not too far away Farm and Fleet store.

It may sound like rugged terrain and conditions, too undesirable to leave sheltered city life for the great outdoors, but it wasn't. It was a great reliever of stress to leave the hustle and bustle and crime of city living. And to experience the natural beauty, the panoramic views of red-white clouds, and blue skies over the mountains and valleys, the clippety-clop of horses crossing the seldom-used paved roads … all irreplaceable experiences of the magnificence and majesty of nature.

Elizabeth and Jack got a boat—not a speed boat but a simple rowboat to enjoy the lake's water that rippled slowly with each stroke of Jack's paddles. They fished, but only to catch and release. They enjoyed all natural outdoor things. They cooked over a campfire and spent most of their time reminiscing and enjoying the mountain views, unavailable to them in Chicago.

It was fitting that Ambrose spent so much time with his parents at the ranch. He helped with all the chores, chopping wood, and fetching water and food for the animals. When he had time alone to paint, he propped his easel to capture the natural beauty of the landscape. His paintings adorned every room of the ranch house.

Jack poured over his books and files to teach Junior and Amanda what they needed to know to be successful in their law practice, successful in their lives' work. It was his almost forgotten son, Ambrose, that would become the best example of life's success. He didn't need a book to teach his parents what was important in life. He did it with art. The art of awareness of what should or should not be, the beauty of being good and doing the right things. Ambrose turned out to be his father's mentor.

It was about time for a family get-together one pleasant weekend in May. Wildflowers were in bloom, and Ambrose, Elizabeth, and Jack finished all their springtime chores to get everything ready for the visit. It was good for Junior and Amanda to join Ambrose to see their parents so relaxed and happy. Jack went shopping for a ham to cook and serve for their gathering. He winced as he purchased the meat that he knew would be required for Junior and Amanda, who had not transitioned to eating grass. Jack, Jr., however, would have to carve the precooked pig.

"Sit here, Ambrose," Jack said, directing Ambrose to the head of the table. "You have been a great help around here and have been inspirational for us to see our lives in the right perspective.

"You *all* have made us very proud, and we hope you all enjoy your lives with great success and happiness. A toast to all!" Jack exclaimed while raising his glass of vintage wine.

After a welcoming meal that would feed royalty and a weekend of fishing and singing campfire songs, Ambrose joined Junior and Amanda in their journey back home to Chicago, where Junior and Amanda had cases waiting for their attention and Ambrose was organizing a march on city hall to protest about things that matter. They all dedicated themselves to their self-chosen careers to serve justice, to pursue the ever-elusive democratic dream of *"liberty and justice for all."*

Theodor Adorno
Philosopher and author,
The Authoritarian Personality

Frankfurt, Germany, 1903–1969

"The phrase, 'the world wants to be deceived,' has become truer than had ever been intended. People are not only, as the saying goes, falling for the swindle; if it guarantees them even the most fleeting gratification, they desire a deception which is nonetheless transparent to them. They force their eyes shut and voice approval, in a kind of self-loathing, for what is meted out to them, knowing fully the purpose for which it is manufactured. Without admitting it they sense that their lives would be completely intolerable as soon as they no longer clung to satisfactions which are none at all."

– Adorno, *Culture Industry Reconsidered*

Aristocles "Plato"
Student of Socrates and
Teacher of Aristotle,
The Republic

Athens, Greece, 428–347 BC

"Until philosophers are kings, or the kings and princes of the world have the spirit and power of philosophy, and a political greatness and wisdom meet in one, and those commoner natures who pursue either to the exclusion of the other are compelled to stand aside, cities will never rest from their evils—no, nor the human race, as I believe—and then only will this our State have a possibility of life and behold the light of day."

– Plato, *Republic, Book V, Just Society*

Patrolman Bruce Norman Garrison / Star #14775

Patrolman William Charles Marsek / Star #14086

KILLED IN LINE OF DUTY

1974 ARTICLE REPRINT   CHICAGO POLICE
MEMORIAL FOUNDATION

Patrolman Bruce Norman Garrison, Star #14775, aged 28 years, was a 3-year, 8-month, 12-day veteran of the Chicago Police Department, assigned to the Bureau of Operational Services – Patrol Division: Unit 056 – Area 6 Special Operations Group.

Patrolman William Charles Marsek, Star #14086, aged 28 years, was a 4-year, 11-month, 24-day veteran of the Chicago Police Department, assigned to the Bureau of Operational Services – Patrol Division: Unit 056 – Area 6 Special Operations Group.

On February 27, 1974, at 8:15 p.m., Patrolmen Bruce Norman Garrison and William Charles Marsek were working the third watch on beat 6653. They were participating in a manhunt for Jacob Paul Cohen, alias Paul Robson, age 30, of 5317 North Wayne, who was wanted for an earlier escape after he was arrested for murder. They observed Cohen emerge from Raven's Pub located at 1818 West Foster Avenue. Cohen walked to his car and then after seeing the officers reentered the tavern. As

Officers Garrison and Marsek investigated, they noticed a sawed-off shotgun near the man's car.

When the officers entered the tavern looking for Cohen, they could not see him because of the poor lighting. As the officers moved further inside, they located Cohen and a struggle ensued. Shots were fired by Cohen. A 10-1 was called and units responded from the 20th District. Officers Garrison and Marsek were both shot in the head and Officer Marsek was also shot in the shoulder and abdomen. Cohen fled out the front door of the tavern and a manhunt ensued. Information was received that Cohen fled in a "beat up" 1964 Rambler, but it was not certain whether he fled in a car or on foot. Police were seen searching the bushes with flashlights in the 5100 block of North Leavitt Avenue and in Winnemac Park.

The gunman made good his escape. Officer Garrison's .38 caliber revolver was missing, and it was believed that Cohen had gained control of the revolver during the struggle and shot both officers with it. Officers Garrison was transported to Ravenswood Hospital where he was pronounced dead at 8:20 p.m. on February 27, 1974. Officer Marsek was transported to Edgewater Hospital where he was pronounced dead at 8:20 p.m. on February 27, 1974.

Jacob Cohen fled to Wisconsin and had told a close female friend his new address and alias he was using to hide out. That friend quickly passed the information on to another male friend and unwittingly betrayed Cohen's trust. Unbeknownst to the female, the male friend was a close friend with Sergeant Thomas Kelly of the Robbery Unit. Sergeant Kelly then relayed the information to Sergeant Rocco Rinaldi of the Homicide Unit. On March 4, 1974, Sergeant Rinaldi alerted the FBI in Milwaukee. Surveillance was set up on Cohen while the two sergeants sped up to Milwaukee to make the arrest. However, Cohen detected the FBI surveillance and shot his way out of the building, wounding Agent Richard Carr. Cohen took refuge in a nearby house and took four children hostage and used one as a shield from bullets while demanding a getaway car. When the child broke free Milwaukee Police and Federal Agents opened fire and Cohen was killed in a hail of gunfire. Cohen sustained 16 gunshot wounds.

Warren J. Breslin
Chicago Police Officer –
The Early Days

Thanks to our troops
for keeping America safe.

We will always remember
your sacrifice for us.

CPSIA information can be obtained
at www.ICGtesting.com
Printed in the USA
BVHW040229210722
642474BV00030B/719/J

9 781977 253668